AN ENCHANTRESS
AWAKENS
Novella

AS THE MOON FALLS

KRISTEN R. MOORE

Midnight Tide
PUBLISHING

As The Moon Falls
Copyright © 2024 Kristen R. Moore

Published by Midnight Tide Publishing
www.midnighttidepublishing.com

Cover design by nox.benedicta.art

Interior Formatting by Book Savvy Services

Edited by Brit Corley

mechanical, or other means now known or hereafter invented, are forbidden without the written permission of the writer or publisher.

Kirsgard Mountains
The Wicked Woods
Wickersham
Davenport
Galdosa River
Copenspire
S. Trinity Forest

Valebridge
Ramshire
Holden Sea
N

Author's Note

Dear reader,

Before you begin your journey under the snow-clad mountains and forests of Teravie, please know that while this story takes place approximately four years before the events of Through the Wicked Wood, it is not intended to be read as a prequel. So, if you have not yet read *Through the Wicked Wood*, stop here and go read that (please!). Then, find your way back and cozy up for this sweet and short enemies to lovers novella.

Happy reading,
Kristen

TRIGGER WARNINGS

Alcoholism, withdrawals, violence, sexual content, consumption of alcohol and tobacco, occasional cursing

For the girls with a quiet voice and a loud mind.
Let me remind you; your softness is your strength.

ONE

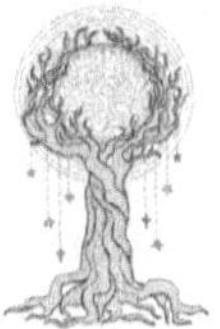

THE IVY TALLULAH PLANTED IN THE GREENHOUSE last year had spread like a fire of green, cascading over the walls and tumbling across the broken stone floor. She never wanted the leafy vines to take up so much of her space, but once they took root, she couldn't stop the determined foliage. And without the use of magick to control the plant, she had to care for it the common way.

With her hands.

It had been a long day and an even longer year.

Tallulah sighed as she reclined against the glass walls of the greenhouse. It'd be so much easier for her magick to cease the growth of the invasive ivy, but it wasn't worth the risk of King Roman's hunters finding her. So, instead, she spent the last few days plucking and trimming the vines, making sure it didn't disrupt the growth of her camellias and the small patch of tomatoes she'd kept alive through the Winter.

Her back ached, but still she kept her position upon the stone floor, glancing at the stubborn greenery, remembering a time only a year ago when she could flick her wrist and command any plant to conjure or cease.

Fleeing Valebridge when King Roman took the throne

began a tumultuous journey of self-discovery. She'd had to learn to hunt her own food. To cook it. To clean up. All the things living in Valebridge with her established family had spoiled her with. But they were gone; the memory of them as tangled and frustrating as the ivy itself.

Tallulah rubbed her temples, the dirt on her hands leaving its mark. She rolled her shoulders and stretched her neck. Clearing the ivy might have been daunting, but it was healing, in its way.

Not that she was ungrateful for her parents and the comforts they'd provided, but when you spend your whole life being treated as a burden, you begin to think as such. And now she'd learned to be on her own; learned maybe she wasn't a burden at all. That maybe she spent the better part of her life believing falsehoods from people whose goal was to keep her under them. To make her feel less than so they could feel more.

She picked at the dirt under her nails. She would certainly need a bath after today. A luxury she was grateful to still have since Enchantresses became hunted.

She was lucky to get out of Valebridge when she did and even luckier to find refuge there, in the northern Trinity Forest. Not far from the bustling city of Davenport, but far enough she could conceal herself.

"What use was a Florecas to a king, anyway?" she grumbled under her breath. She tossed her dirty trowel into her bucket, the clang of the metal ringing out in the silent space.

Tallulah attributed her use to the king as to the reason they hadn't found her. She supposed it wasn't that important to anyone. And she was fine with it. Glad, even, to have magick no one cared for.

But she missed it terribly. Every day she spent here added another layer of dust to her memory and use of magick.

She chuckled at the irony of being a Florecas living in a greenhouse. The need to worship all of Mother Gaia's living things was in her blood, but *especially* as a Florecas—the ability to make plants grow and move and change was at the very root of who she was.

When she'd stumbled upon the broken-down greenhouse, she knew it was where she belonged. A gift from Mother Gaia, perhaps. The forest had concealed most of it. Moss growing around the sides, thick trees lined around the building creating an almost cocoon made of earth.

And because she'd been diligent about not using her magick, she remained unseen by any of the hunters.

Her eyes wandered the now low lit room, smiling at the copious amounts of plants and flowers.

Being a Florecas in a world that demands power and destruction wasn't easy. Her mother must've been disappointed, being a Healer with a Florecas for a daughter. Maybe that's why she treated her as low as the dirt in which her plants grew.

But there was power in the soil. Without it, there wouldn't be *this*.

She glanced around the room again. At the life that was exploding around her despite the unusually cold weather happening just outside the greenhouse doors. Rich greens and vibrant purples scattered the tabletops and workbenches. Tomatoes, full and juicy for picking in the dead of Winter. How is *that* not miraculous?

Her mother was never her friend. Never her ally. Of course, she was desperate for her approval.

She never got it.

Whenever she felt the pull of being less than, of being unimportant, of being a *disappointment*, all she did was look around this room. Though she grew these plants from seedlings, and not her magick, there was still a sense of pride, of accomplishment.

Even the pesky ivy.

Slowly, she stood, interlocking her fingers in front of her outstretched arms to regain feeling in them. Her body was stiff after the day's work, and nothing sounded better than crawling into her basin and submerging herself.

She took a final glance at the room, a smile dancing along her lips. The creeping vines aside, the greenhouse was still mostly glass. Walls that jutted toward the massive dome ceiling were speckled with greenery and occasional bursts of color from the dahlias. However, the ceiling remained free of any foliage; she made sure of that.

Her favorite part of the day was when the sun crested in the sky and cascaded down through the room in the early morning. Drips of orange and pink filtering through each glassy pane until it reached down and shone upon her plants.

Dusk had settled over the forest, and the moon and sun battled for space in the cold, Winter sky. She let out another long sigh before heading to her wash basin.

Once out of the bath, she tossed her sweat and dirt-ridden blouse and pants in a pile in the corner and switched instead to a cotton, ivory nightgown. Curling up on the sofa, she pulled the wool blanket up to her chin. Images of ivy danced in her head as she tumbled off into a deep sleep.

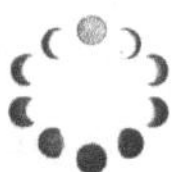

THE SUN SAT low in the sky, tickling Tallulah's skin as she walked through the snowy trees the next morning. Just over a year she'd had been here and had yet to meet anyone else. To be careful, she always masked her eyes. Concealing the otherworldly blue they naturally were, to a soft brown instead. Sending a silent prayer to the Mother that today would be just like any day spent in the forest; uneventful.

It didn't take long before the birds found her. They always did. Their song bright and cheery despite the freezing wind that was stirring. "Hello, little ones," she whispered. "You're up early." The bluebirds landed upon her outstretched hand and sang their lovely tune. She smiled as the birds took flight together toward the riverbank.

The water was almost unbearable to touch, but luckily hadn't frozen over. She yanked on her trap. The basket shot to the surface with a violent splash of icy water. Though empty, she didn't feel disappointed. She knew better. Mother Gaia had always looked after her, and today would be no different. Empty basket or not. She shrugged and placed the trap back, then headed for the clearing nearby where she'd laid a trap. Perhaps she could harvest some leftover beargrass from Autumn. It wasn't the most pleasant to eat, but it filled her stomach, and she couldn't afford to be choosy.

Halfway to the clearing, a shriek pierced the air. Tallulah halted in her tracks, the crunching of snow beneath her boots silenced as white puffs expelled with each breath.

Another shriek.

"Leave me alone!"

Tallulah froze. She spun on her heels and dropped her body low to the snowy ground.

Who was out here? No one was *ever* out here, especially in Winter. Davenport was a few miles away, but the merchant ships should've long since passed and the townspeople knew better than to get caught in this kind of cold. The best hunting was done on the opposite side of the forest. She'd ventured there once, only to be greeted by a group of men. Luckily, they didn't see her, too caught up on their most recent kill to notice an onlooker.

"Please let me go!"

The child's screams raised the hairs on the back of Tallulah's neck.

It is your duty to serve and protect the lives of those who live in Teravie.

Her memory drifted back to her schooling in Valebridge. How Enchantresses were an extension of Mother Gaia, and by being born with the gift of magick, it was her duty to help those without.

Except, they'd banned her magick and hunted Enchantresses. Lies spun and twisted by King Roman.

If she were to help, they'd see her. And if she were to be seen, she'd no longer be safe here. Her heart twisted into a tight ball, constricting, and pulling in each direction. Despite the gnawing feeling in her gut to turn and run, she'd decided it was in her blood to help, and so help, she must.

Leaving her basket, Tallulah sprinted through the clearing, toward the screams. Her feet carried her swiftly through the frozen grass, past the evergreen trees shrouded in white, until she reached the line where the forest met the sea. Crashing waves sounded from the side of the cliff while deep green pine trees towered to the left. And there, in the middle of it all, she saw what she dreaded most.

Royal Hunters.

Men employed to track down Enchantresses and bring them to Valebridge for a handsome bounty.

The men took turns shoving a small boy back and forth. Her lip curled. The boy couldn't be over ten years. His face was dirty, his feet bare. *He must be freezing*. She clenched her fists at her sides, the rage in her heart multiplying by the second.

"Leave me be!" the boy shouted again, but the men were relentless. The image of King Roman's grizzly bear displayed proudly on each of their cloaks.

"Tell us where to find her, and we'll let you live," a hunter snarled. He was a big man, both in height and in stature.

Her stomach dropped. She recognized that young boy from last Spring. He'd stumbled upon her garden shed next to the greenhouse. He didn't ask questions, didn't pry when he found her digging up the bugleweed that grew around the area. She'd sent him off with a bouquet from her garden to take to his mother and a basket of tomatoes and carrots. He looked hungry then, now he looked starved.

The men twisted and turned the boy's arms at an unnatural angle. They had weapons at their sides, but Tallulah wasn't afraid. Her body shook. Her jaw ached from being clenched so tightly.

"I told you already," the boy screamed. "I haven't seen any witch around here!"

Witch. Tallulah scoffed. If only she were a forest witch, mixing simple potions and casting wards, then maybe she'd lead a more normal life. Blend in with the rest of the humans. But alas, she was not. She couldn't even use her magick to ward her greenhouse without the risk of hunters sensing her.

The boy shrieked again. Tallulah blinked, ripped back to the present. The hunters twisted his arms back, much too far. His yelps filled the forest and his pleads landed right in Tallulah's heart. Without thought, she did something she hadn't done since finding refuge in the greenhouse. Fingers flexing, she raised her wrists and called upon her magick.

She wasn't entirely sure if it would come, given its restful state over the last year. It took only a moment before the vines flowed freely from her palms. Twisting and turning, the plant she despised yesterday now seemed like the perfect weapon.

The ivy snaked from her palms, carving a line in the snow, over the dirt and up the bodies of the hunters before they knew she was even there. Their eyes widened, their arms dropping from the boy. He met her eye briefly, giving her a quick nod before sprinting through the wood.

Tallulah stepped closer, letting her rage flow through the ivy, tightening around each of the hunter's necks. She pictured King Roman, her heart maddened at the fate of the Enchantresses across Teravie. She squeezed and squeezed until the men's faces were red. And then blue.

Their eyes bulged, and their mouths moved in soundless pleas. And then she stopped. Not able to bring herself to kill them, she retracted the ivy she'd summoned. It swirled through the grass and back into her palms as if it'd never been there at all.

Both men dropped in tandem, gasping and choking for air. Before they could get a sense of what happened, she was running.

Back to her greenhouse.

To her sanctuary.

She made sure to run a few circles, dragging her feet through the snow to not leave a clear path before she bolted through the door and latched it shut.

Her breathing was heavy and her heartbeat relentless. But she didn't care. Tallulah sank onto the stone floor, clenching her fists tightly. She'd used her magick. She should be afraid. Ashamed for hurting those men and yet, a smile spread across her face as bright and wild as the ivy she conjured. She brought her hands to her chest, clasping them tight. Maybe being a Florecas wasn't so useless after all.

Two

"Next!" the royal guard yelled.

Evren found it odd that the Blackwind Tavern was where they had the recruits sworn in. Davenport had always been a meeting ground for the Royal Hunters, but the tavern his men had chosen was dark and reeked of debauchery. He'd been here many times in his youth, having grown up just outside the port city. It wasn't a tavern to brag about, with its dim lights and poor selection of ale.

He fiddled with the rim of his glass, and another man stepped forward, his black boots heavy against the ale-stained wooden floors. It should've been Evren swearing the new hunters in tonight, but he was tired and Markus was all too eager to take his place. So, he found a corner to sink into while he kept his eyes locked on the recruits.

"Joseph, do you swear to uphold your oath to the crown? To aid in the hunt for magick across Teravie. To bring each Enchantress you find to Valebridge, alive, as demanded by King Roman himself." Markus paused, and it took the recruit, Joseph, a moment to realize it was because he waited for an answer.

He cleared his throat and met Markus' eye. "Yes."

Evren smiled as he lifted his ale and took a long sip. His lips puckered at the sour taste. He much preferred whisky, but this late in the season provisions were minimal. At the end of the day, it didn't matter what he drank, as long as he was drinking.

"And do you swear to take your tonic daily, to ensure not to miss the use of magick?" Markus' voice boomed over the loud patrons playing a lively game of cards in the back of the tavern.

"Yes," Joseph said with haste. Evren chuckled. *The recruits are always so eager to please.*

Evren wasn't keen about taking the tonic. It left a bitter taste in his mouth and an even worse headache the next day. But it certainly worked. He'd had much success the last year finding Enchantresses who'd escaped Valebridge and the tonic he took tugged him right to them.

He'd found six Enchantresses in hiding last year. Six bounties, six payouts. And all he needed was one more. One more catch and he'd be free.

Joining the royal hunt was the out he'd been looking for after his injury. A Healer turned on him on the day of the uprising, using her magick to snap his leg in three places, leaving him unable to continue as Captain of the Royal Guard and since then he'd felt lost.

A dull ache flashed through his leg at the memory. Shrugging it off, he took another sip of ale.

He'd found his new place as the headhunter of King Roman's new Royal Hunters. All he needed was to acquire one more Enchantress, pocket his coin, and board a ship that would take him far, far away from here. Far away from the responsibilities of home looming over his shoulder.

"I officially announce you, Joseph Huxham, as a royal hunter for King Roman." Markus pinned a grizzly badge to the recruit's wool vest.

Joseph turned toward Evren.

The kid couldn't be over eighteen. His bright hazel eyes lit up as Evren nodded his approval. *Just a boy.*

"Thank you, Captain Fletcher," Joseph said.

He stepped back in line with the rest of the men. Something in Evren's stomach sank at the title. *Captain.* He hadn't been a true captain in a year. Not since his injury, but the name stuck; the men respected him more for it.

Markus dismissed the recruits. He moved through the tables, dipping his head at the patrons, clapping a few on their backs. Evren envied his easy nature and scowled into his cup. They'd grown up together, spending their youth on the docks of Davenport and fishing in the Holden Sea. That is, before Evren left for Valebridge. Markus had stayed behind, helping his father run the family farm.

"Can't wait to get my first catch," Markus whispered and slid into the booth. A hunter for only a month, but he'd proven a great asset. One Evren would be remiss without.

Evren poured his friend a tall tankard of ale from the pitcher on the table and handed him the glass.

"The coin alone is going to change everything, Ev. But the thrill of the hunt—" He let out a low whistle. "Can't wait to get my hands on those filthy women."

Evren smiled. He wished he shared the same enthusiasm. Even though hunting had been fruitful, he grew tired of the regime. A permanent knot had formed in the pit of his stomach with every Enchantress he delivered to Valebridge. He pushed the feeling aside, focusing on his friend. Markus' blonde hair glinted under the dim light of the tavern. His dark eyes, much like the eyes of his father, were watchful. Mischievous.

"There has to be some hiding in the forest, don't you think?"

Evren shrugged. "It's likely, but there's a storm coming. Might make things more difficult."

Markus laughed before finishing off his drink. "Won't stop me." He winked.

Markus had always been the one coming up with schemes. Plans. Pranks. In fact, it was he who suggested Evren join the

Royal Hunters after his injury. Evren pushed back at first, not caring enough to spend his days looking for Enchantresses. Not wanting to give them an ounce of his time after what they'd done to his leg. But without any other options, he accepted the position offered by King Roman, and almost a year later, Markus was finally able to join him.

The shillings being offered for a single Enchantress were life changing. Two hundred shillings a head. That kind of coin would let Evren and Markus embark on a new journey. A new life. A dream they both had since they were young boys. To travel. See all the world had to offer. To leave the responsibilities donned upon them from birth and pave their own way.

"Time for some tonics." Markus took a quick sip of ale before standing and opening the wooden box that contained the vials.

"Let me." Evren stood and grabbed the box from Markus to distribute them. He rubbed the small glass vial between his thumb before passing them out.

With every vial handed to the men, they met him with a precise, "Thank you, Captain Fletcher." His stomach dropped each time. *Captain, captain.* A constant reminder of who he no longer was.

As he settled back into his booth with Markus, the two of them raised their vials in a sort of cheers before tossing back the ruby liquid. The taste of the tonic was just as awful as he remembered, so he chugged several large gulps of ale to chase it down.

"You sure that's a good idea?" Markus gestured to the pint in Evren's hand.

He hadn't always had a problem with the drink, but after his injury he found himself relying on an escape more and more frequently. It had gotten out of hand a few months back and he found himself being dragged to his uncle's estate to recover. It had taken six long days for the slew of ale to leave his system. One hundred and forty four tortuous hours of vomiting, and cold sweats. He thought, surely, this would convince him to never lift a tankard again. And yet, his mind seemed to forget completely the hell he went through to get the ale out of his body. The moment he walked past the Blackwind Tavern, all hope was lost as he downed ale after ale.

Evren ignored Markus, his eyes roaming the tavern instead. Black iron lanterns skirted along the walls, giving the room a soft amber glow. Several tables and booths were placed across the floor, rounded wooden tops all the same. Each of the recruits were still there, celebrating and toasting each other as if they were doing some sort of good for Teravie.

Perhaps they were. Evren had witnessed firsthand how powerful Enchantresses could be. His leg ached again at the memory. He held in a shudder remembering the look of fear each woman wore as he dragged them to the king and instead focused on his friend.

"I'm fine," Evren finally said, taking another sip of his ale. "I can manage just one." The lie felt sour in his mouth, but he didn't need Markus to worry about him. Not tonight, not ever. He didn't face Markus again as he tipped the pint to his lips and drank it in its entirety.

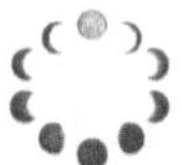

ADMITTEDLY, Evren had one too many drinks. Once he had the sip of the first, he couldn't stop. Didn't want to. He waited until Markus left for his room at the Lonely Seabird Inn before he ordered another ale. Then another. And another.

"You okay?" Markus asked, popping his head out of his adjacent room, likely hearing Evren stumble up the stairs.

Evren tripped on the last step but righted himself before Markus could make a move toward him. "Fine," Evren mumbled, before slamming his door shut.

Evren awoke the next morning with a soreness behind his

eyes and disappointment lining his stomach. He knew better than to drink the day before a hunt. He knew better than to drink *at all*, but he couldn't help it. The way the ale soothed the constant itch of worry under his skin was addicting. He would never tell Markus, but he couldn't remember the last time he went without a drink. And the shame of it only drew him to drink more.

After washing, Evren changed into his dark brown pants, matching linen shirt, and heavy gray wool cloak. He ran his fingers over the grizzly badge pinned to his chest before fastening the clasp at his neck. Not quite the same crest he wore as a royal guard, but a sense of pride filled him, anyway.

He'd taken matters into his hands after his injury and was determined to make a new life. His mind flashed briefly to training with his uncle throughout his childhood. How pride had filled him then, too, when he learned what he'd inherit. Of the role he would play for his country.

Now the thought made him sick. The last thing he wanted was to be rooted in Teravie, stuck on a makeshift throne overseeing the Trinity Forest.

All he had to do was find one more Enchantress, and he'd be free of the burden.

"I'm headed toward Copenspire this morning," Markus said as they ate their breakfast back at the Blackwind Tavern. "You were right about that storm. It's closing in and best to get through the forest before the snow starts. You should come with me, more likely to find one of them if we work together."

"Maybe," Evren said and took another bite of his porridge. "But I have to go to see my uncle sooner than later. I'll just catch up with you after."

"Oh shite," Markus groaned, running a hand down his face. "I forgot about that"

"Yeah, it's about time." Evren didn't hate his uncle. But he *did* hate that he didn't have any heirs. So, the next in line for the Lord of the Jade Guild fell to him. He didn't want the title anymore. Didn't want the responsibility to look after an entire region of Teravie when he hardly felt adequate to take care of himself.

The thought of spending his life trapped in the forest where he grew up devastated him.

They finished their porridge in silence, the occasional slurping and clatter of utensils filling the space.

Markus pushed his bowl to the side and leaned back in his seat. "Well, fine. Meet me in Copenspire when the storm passes, I bet if there's Enchantresses hiding, it's gotta be near there. I've heard rumors of them fleeing to the mountains."

Evren nodded his agreement. He would gladly meet Markus in Copenspire, just after he confronted his uncle to let him know he wouldn't be taking over the Jade Guild any time soon as planned. Or ever.

"And if you need anything, Ev–"

"I told you I'm fine, Markus," Evren snapped. The spinning in his head worsened. The call for ale while they sat in the tavern, distracting.

Markus watched him, his dark eyes scouring Evren's face before he nodded and rose from the table. He clasped his shoulder, giving it a quick squeeze as he walked by.

THE SUN WAS beautiful this morning despite the bitter cold. Plus, the first full moon of Winter was tonight. Evren had had luck the past year finding Enchantresses on the night of the full moons. Perhaps tonight would be no different.

He pulled his flask from his coat pocket, blessing the barkeep for pulling a dusty bottle of whisky from the larder before he'd left the tavern. His shoulders unclenched as the liquid settled warm in his belly.

Walking out of the city proper, Evren found himself among

the snow-laden trees of the Trinity Forest that edged along Davenport. He'd spent so much of his life lost in the woods of the Jade Guild. Running and climbing, living freely and wild as children should.

The trees were different today. Their branches were heavier, not just from the snow. The wind hissed, blowing mists of white into his path. He continued his trek with no destination in mind when he halted in the middle of the forest, clutching his stomach. Something tugged at his middle. Pulling him to the east, farther away from Davenport.

He recognized the feeling immediately. The tug and pull in the core of his being, guiding him to *magick*. The tonic he drank last night, bitter and foul, now tasted like freedom. His feet moved, his instincts heightened, and he followed that tug all the way to the edge of the forest, where he found two hunters gasping for air on the icy ground.

THREE

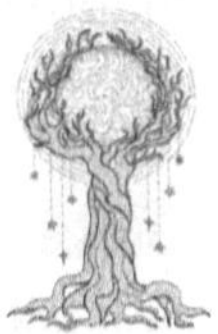

AFTER THE ENCOUNTER WITH THE HUNTERS EARLIER that morning, Tallulah felt somehow more confident than she ever had in her life and equally more terrified.

Never once had she used her magick in that way to save someone. She also had never used her magick to hurt anyone, either. She was always told a Florecas had no other purpose than tending to the royal gardens and grounds. But now she saw her magick for what it really was.

A weapon.

She mourned briefly, thinking of all the Enchantresses she could've saved in Valebridge before she'd fled. If she'd thought to use her magick this way, she could have been more useful. She brushed the thought aside, knowing it wouldn't do well to dwell on the past.

The sun had breached high in the sky by the time she was bold enough to venture out of the greenhouse. Her water supply was low, and since she abandoned her morning chores early, she needed to fetch her rain buckets. They were likely frozen from the dropping temperatures, and it would take time and patience for them to thaw.

The glass door of the greenhouse creaked as it opened.

She peered through the sliver of a crack before opening it farther. The sun remained covered behind thick, white clouds, but the brightness of the snow made her squint through the doorway.

When she didn't hear anything out of the ordinary, no hunters chattering, no weapons being drawn, she piled up her long sage skirt and stepped out into the snow.

Tallulah spotted the buckets right where she left them against the back of the small storage shed next to the greenhouse. The mossy covered roof was now painted white. The wind whipped at her cheeks as she trekked across the grounds toward the buckets.

She tugged the first one forward and huffed out a labored breath, wiping the cold sweat from her forehead. It was heavy from being frozen solid. She'd have to come back for the other.

As her boots crunched atop the frozen snow, something in the air heightened her senses. The wind picked up again, whipping her dark strands into her eyes, biting her cheeks and bringing forth a few rogue tears. But something was wrong.

Off.

Abandoning the bucket, she sprinted toward the greenhouse, hoping whatever watched would miss her completely. She let out a sigh of relief when she reached for the door.

A heavy hand wrapped around her arm, her scream frozen in her throat.

"I don't think so, Enchantress," a gruff voice said behind her.

She whipped her head. Every small moment of her life the last year raced through her mind. The greenhouse and the birds. The seedlings and the ivy. Every small accomplishment threatened to vanish in an instant. Her eyes snagged on the grizzly badge pinned perfectly on the man's chest, parallel to her face. Then she tipped her eyes upward.

"You're coming with me," the man said, his green eyes holding such malice. Such hate.

"I would advise you to let me go," Tallulah said. Though her insides shook, she held her body strong.

She scoured his face, looking for any sign of remorse. All she was met with was scrutiny. Judgment reflected in those forest green eyes. His nose and cheeks smattered with freckles that matched the color of his dark auburn hair. She tugged her arm, attempting to free herself from his grip.

"You can fight all you want, but you're coming with me either way. So, I'd save some strength for Valebridge if I were you." She shivered, her skin growing colder by the second, not just from the storm fast approaching.

She wriggled her arm again, but with each movement, his grip grew tighter. His eyes narrowed, and he used his free hand to grab something from his belt. The clinking of iron shackles rang in her ears and again all those little moments raced through her mind.

Once the shackles are in place, I'll have no chance of using my magick.

She flexed the fingers on her free hand and called upon the ivy, just as she did earlier this morning. She kept the rest of her body perfectly still, watching the man, and moved her fingers slightly. Urging the vines to come forth, coaxing them out little by little.

The vines slid silently over the top of his boots just as he got the shackles free from his belt. Turning to her, he smiled, a cruel, wicked smile, and slammed the first shackle around her wrist. His arrogance shone in his features.

But he was too late.

The ivy at his feet tightened abruptly with one swish of Tallulah's free wrist, and before he could come to terms with what was happening, he slammed hard into the frozen ground.

"Fuck!" He cupped the back of his head. If he was angry before, he was completely enraged now. "Stay where you—"

Tallulah swished her wrist, sending the ivy farther up around his neck and over his mouth. She clenched her fist, a mix of terror and adrenaline rushing through her as she took down a third hunter in less than a few hours.

The man gasped for air, clawing at the green vines that grew tighter and tighter around his mouth before his eyes rolled back, and he stopped moving.

Tallulah stilled. Watching him, waiting for him to wake up. Crouching to his side, she focused on his chest for any movement. There was none.

Her breaths came in short spurts, her chest tightening. She hadn't meant to kill him, even though a small part of her thought he deserved it. She pressed her palms to his chest, the iron around her wrist clanking loudly as she bent down. Blowing out a long breath, she relaxed back on her heels. The ends of her dress soaked from the snow.

Breathing.

He was still breathing. She had only rendered him unconscious. Her relief lasted only moments. Her eyes widened. She had an even bigger problem. She'd used her magick again and surely more men would be nearby. Not to mention, she now had an unconscious hunter to dispose of.

FOUR

This was the second time in a row Evren had woken up with a sore head. But this was different. A deep ache set in the back of his skull. How much had he had to drink this time? He groaned as the fog in his mind lifted. Where had he been yesterday? Where was he now?

His room at the inn was small, unimpressive, and dark. But when he opened his eyes now, the first thing he saw took his breath away. Stars danced above him through a large, domed glass ceiling. The moon was high and bright, as full as she'd get in the sky. He was lost momentarily in the beauty of his new surroundings. The glass and the stars and the silver light of the moon.

His eyes drifted lower to the rest of the room. Ivy hung heavily on nearly every surface. Thick and green and shimmering under the moonlight. Something about it felt familiar. Something about it...

He surged forward, attempting to stand up, only to realize he couldn't. His body struggled against the vines that tightened around his middle and his arms, tying him securely to a wooden workbench in a corner. His wrists, bound by his own iron shackles, were useless behind his back. He wriggled again; the plants moaning but not snapping as he pushed and pulled to free himself.

"You're wasting your time," a soft voice said from somewhere he couldn't locate. "Those vines won't move, won't break unless I tell them to."

His memory slammed back into him with full force. Pounding, viscous images of the events that transpired after he parted ways with Markus.

He'd found those two hunters gasping for air near the clearing by the cliffs. Had helped them back to Davenport and then resumed his hunt. He then followed that tug in his stomach until it led him to a small storage shed in the forest.

Evren didn't notice the greenhouse at first. Its rounded shape covered in snow was easily bypassed. But he noticed her right away, and yet, he'd hesitated. He'd taken his time pulling the shackles from his pocket and, with that fraction of a moment, everything changed.

The Enchantress stepped into view, drawing his attention. The light of the moon illuminated her sharp features. Her dark hair hung loosely well past her shoulders, her tan skin glowing in the silver light. Her eyes, the brightest blue he'd ever seen, were narrowed at him. The sage dress hanging loosely from her body was ripped on the bottom, the seams coming undone. Though it still snugged on her hips—

She cleared her throat and heat flooded Evren's cheeks when he realized where his gaze had landed.

"You've made a grave mistake, Enchantress." Evren focused on the ivy that still gripped him. "Others will sense your magick, you won't stay hidden for long."

Others would come, wouldn't they? He wasn't so sure. The men he'd helped back to Davenport were sure to come looking for the woman who disabled them, unless they were too cowardly to seek her out. They weren't even coherent enough to interrogate, so there was a chance they wouldn't remember what happened at all.

But then there was Markus.

Shite. Markus had already left for Copenspire, and they weren't to meet for several weeks.

His eyes dragged back to the Enchantress. She'd moved fully from the shadows and perched herself on the velvet sofa in the middle of the room, bringing her knees to her chest. Her eyes scanned every inch of him, making his blood boil. This was his moment, his chance to capture one last of these despicable creatures and collect his coin, and she had foiled it all.

Though she wasn't despicable. Not in a literal sense. He hated the thought as soon as it entered his mind.

She's bewitching you, you idiot. So, he pushed the thought further away, forcing himself to see her for what she really was. A monster.

"What's your plan, then?" Evren spat, forgoing any more attempts to free himself. "Kill me? Keep me captive? Sacrifice me to this apparent Mother Gaia?"

The woman scoffed. "Apparent?"

Evren shrugged the best he could, being tied down. "You all believe in some imaginary figure. You give your life to her and for what? For this?"

He looked around the greenhouse, noting how little she had to her name other than the ridiculous abundance of plants.

Her eyes narrowed further. "And who is it you worship, hunter?"

He leaned forward, the plants groaning under the strain. "No one," he hissed.

A flash of hurt shot across her face before she shook it off, running her fingers through her dark hair.

"What was *your* plan?" she asked, crossing her arms and straightening her legs. The long sleeves of her dress dangled loosely off her arms.

How did he get into this predicament? How embarrassing would it be when he finally brought her in, having to explain why it took so long? Because he *would* bring her in, he had no doubt about that. If only he could get out of these vines...

"Have you forgotten how to speak?" The woman stood, rounding the end of the sofa, and kneeled before him where he was tied to the workbench. Her face was only inches from his, her dark brows furrowed.

"My plan was to take you back to Valebridge where you belong," Evren said, anger rising in his chest. The audacity of this Enchantress to speak to him so casually. He kept his movements slow as his fingers began working, a knotted vine wrapped around his back.

The woman's brows furrowed farther as she stood again and backed away from him.

"Now tell me, Enchantress, what will you do with me?" He wasn't sure he really wanted the answer. Evil as magick users were, his mind could only imagine the horrors she'd inflict on him inside this greenhouse. It'd been too easy for one of them to snap his leg. And in doing so, ruin his life.

His eyes shot back to the woman, who paced back and forth, her long dress dragging across the broken and dirty stone. Her fingers twitched, and though the light was faint, he could tell she was chewing her bottom lip.

"You don't have a plan," Evren said plainly. Humor tickled him and if he hadn't been tied to a damn bench, he would've laughed.

"What makes you so sure?" The Enchantress stopped her pacing. Evren rolled his head to look at her. Worry splayed across her face, and she tapped her booted foot impatiently.

"You could have easily killed me outside," he said, his anger subsiding momentarily. "Could've left me to be buried in the oncoming snow. To freeze. But you didn't. So, if your plan is to keep me alive, it's a poor one. You'll be caught before you do whatever sinister experiments you're planning."

"Sinister experiments?" Her voice raised as she marched across the stone floor. "Sinister experiments?" she shouted again, flicking her wrists. As she did, the vines around him tightened further, cutting into his abdomen.

"Case and point," he said, his lungs collapsing under the squeeze of the vines. His voice must have broken her rage, because in an instant the vines loosened. As they did, he let out an overdue breath.

"I have no plans for you, hunter." She stomped back the opposite way. "For all I care, you can spend the rest of your days tied to that workbench. It's no matter to me."

And then she was gone, and he was left alone.

FIVE

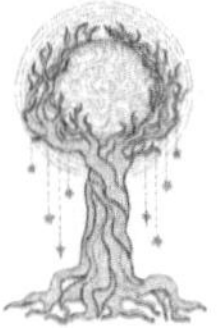

Tallulah took her time before heading back to the main area of the greenhouse. She'd spent the night curled up in her empty water basin, missing the comfort of her sofa, but she couldn't justify being in the same room with that man any longer. She had absolutely no idea what she would do with this hunter. Killing him was out of the question. It went against every fiber of her being. Keeping him here also wouldn't be sustainable.

She supposed she could leave. Pack what little she had and go, hoping by some miracle she'd be long gone before someone found him or he escaped. Sorrow filled her at the thought. The greenhouse was her home when they'd already ripped her actual home from her. She didn't want to see it go to waste by some hunters.

It neared midday when she finally gathered the courage to face the hunter again. Tallulah balanced a basket of food on her hip as she made her way into the domed room. The ivy greeted her, its leaves moving slightly in the same direction she walked. As if it were desperate to be in her proximity.

"So, you *are* still here," the man said, his demeanor less

menacing in the light of day. Or he was just hungry and hopeful she'd brought him something to eat. Of course she had. She wasn't about to let him starve despite his cruelty.

Tallulah ignored him, dropping the basket on the sofa in silence before turning to tend to her plants. The vines she'd placed around the man had loosened, but she paid no mind. Knowing how quickly she could call upon them to tighten if she needed to.

He sat quietly, watching her as she watered row upon row of dahlias, pansies, and clematis. Sweat beaded across the hunter's forehead, his eyes sunken and hazed. Surely it couldn't have been that long since he'd eaten, so something else must be bothering him. Sickness from the cold, perhaps.

She took her time, lazily refilling her watering can, making him sweat further with each silent passing. When her tasks were complete and her plants cared for, she turned to him again.

His green eyes burned into her, his dark auburn hair disheveled, though she got the impression he wasn't typically one to leave a hair out of place. His clothes were immaculate for a hunter, barely any dirt dusted upon his black boots.

"Are you ill?" Tallulah asked. Her voice was calm, though her stomach swirled with unease. She would never let it show. Never let him see just how scared she was of him. She couldn't. That much she knew, never show your fear.

The man eyed her for a moment, his dark brows furrowed, creating a deep crease between them.

"Still reeling from the wound on your head from your fall?" She bit her lip to keep from smiling. He had appeared so intimidating at first, and yet how easily he fell. Of course, she'd stitched him up last night to the best of her abilities while he remained unconscious. She couldn't help herself.

When he said nothing, she let out a dramatic breath. "Are you hungry, then?"

"Do you think I'm daft?" he asked, his voice lifting at the

end like he was on the verge of laughter. "You really believe I'd take food from you, Enchantress? With all these plants, how am I to be sure you haven't poisoned it?"

"I suppose you can't be certain." Heat rose to her cheeks. The thought of poisoning him hadn't even crossed her mind, but now that he'd mentioned it, it didn't sound like such a bad idea. She'd feed him only a little nightshade to make him fall asleep. Then she'd return him to the woods. Dragging his body would certainly take time she couldn't afford... She bit her lip.

He scoffed, shaking his head in laughter. "Not hungry."

She didn't believe him. Tallulah rolled her eyes as she headed toward the basket she left on the sofa.

"Apples, dried deer jerky, and a canteen of water," she said, placing the basket at the man's feet. "I will unshackle one of your hands if you can swear all you'll use it for is to eat."

It was a risk; this she understood. But she could use her magick if she needed it. He flinched as she got closer. His eyes widening as her hands pulled the key from her pocket. She took his silence as an agreement, nodding to him just once before rounding behind him to unshackle one of his hands. She backed away, keeping her eyes on him.

He didn't move.

She waited, her foot tapping on the stone floor, as she watched him. Surely, he was hungry. And if not, *surely*, he'd try to attack her. So she stayed pinned to the greenhouse wall, her hands ready to call upon the ivy if she needed it.

What felt like an eternity later, the hunter bent forward, picking up the basket and placing it on his lap. The crunch of an apple made Tallulah breathe out with a sigh of relief. She wasn't sure why she cared so much that he was fed, but it didn't sit right on her conscience to deny him this.

Once he'd eaten the apple to its core, the hunter turned his head to peer at her over his shoulder.

"Thank you," he whispered before turning back to eat what was left of the basket.

EVREN FINISHED every bit of food the Enchantress left him, forgoing any worry about it being poisoned. If it was, he'd know his fate eventually. Besides, the way his body revolted against the lack of ale was enough to kill him. The food was a momentary distraction, so he didn't care if it she'd poisoned it.

Once finished, he placed the basket back down and she unshackled his other hand to guide him to an area where he could relieve himself. She kept her hands up, her eyes locked on him like a prisoner. It was humiliating.

He made his way back to the workbench, sitting down as she shackled his hands again.

"I'll check on you again come nightfall," the Enchantress said.

"What's your name?" he asked, immediately regretting it. The last thing he should do was get familiar with this Enchantress. But if he got in her good graces, he could somehow get back out of these shackles. Could earn her trust and break free.

She paused in front of him and tucked the basket into her side. Her blue eyes narrowed beneath furrowed, dark brows before her features softened.

"Tallulah Hollow," she said. "And yours, hunter?" She smiled, quick and small, before she must've realized she'd done so. Her face shifted again, back to something more stoic. But he didn't miss the minor change.

"Evren," he said. His hands flexed, the shackles irritating against his skin, and he shifted on the workbench, only now noticing she didn't rebind him as tightly with the ivy. "Evren Fletcher."

"Evren," she repeated quietly. She turned then and headed for the door; the only time since she arrived that she placed her back to him.

This was his chance.

He pushed past the ache in his leg and the swirling of his head and, in an instant, sprung forward from the ground, snapping the ivy in two. Before Tallulah had any clue of what was happening, he placed his shackled hands over her head and pressed tightly against her throat, caging her in front of him against his chest.

She shrieked before the basket hit the ground, and her nails raked against the skin of his forearms.

"Please," she gasped. Scratches lined his arms, the sting deep and sharp. Something caught the corner of his eye and a moment later, the ivy shifted.

No, the ivy lining the walls *leaped* forward, encasing him and the Enchantress.

Evren fell to the ground, and the Enchantress slipped free from his grip. He was lost in a sea of green, buried by the foliage. He grappled to get to his feet, to uncover himself. He ripped the last of the vines covering his face. The Enchantress stood, her face reddened, and her hair a mess of black waves. Her blue eyes striking and cold.

"It would serve you well to remain still," she said through a few breathless pants.

His eyes snagged on the mark around her throat. The mark where his forearm almost ended her life. He moved, but the ivy pressed heavier upon his chest, pinning him in place, wrapping around his ankles and arms.

"I tried to be kind." The look in her eye was feral and mad. "But it seems as though I underestimated your competency."

"Or have *you* overestimated your hiding place?" The weight of the ivy pained his chest and legs. "Keep using that magick of yours, Enchantress. The other hunters will be here in no time."

Her nostrils flared, her face still red with anger. But Evren was always one for details. That's what had made him such a successful hunter and before that, a captain. So, when the single tear fell from the Enchantress' eye, he didn't miss it. She turned away, likely to conceal her moment of weakness. And for whatever reason, his mind twisted with confusion as his stomach sank with guilt.

Six

Idiot. Tallulah couldn't believe she cried in front of this hunter. She'd meant to appear strong, just as her mother would have expected her. Just as the other Enchantresses in Valebridge had been. But Tallulah never felt strong. She felt quiet and soft. All the things that the world disapproved of. All the things that would now get her killed, get her caught.

Of course, it was a terrible idea to trust him. Of course, it was reckless to leave the ivy less tethered around him. Why did she care for his comfort at all? If she were her mother, she would've ended his life in the snow.

But she wasn't.

Evren groaned from behind her, still pinned to the ground with the heavy plants. She wiped her eyes before turning to face him again.

"I'm going to let you up." She took a tentative step. Her throat sore from where he'd choked her, but she pushed past the pain. She needed to be strong.

Be strong. Be strong. Be strong.

"Once I remove the ivy, I will offer you two options."

Evren said nothing as Tallulah's fingers moved, the ivy stirring. His green eyes were bright against the deep red in his hair, his freckles prominent against his pale skin.

"Your first option." Tallulah lifted her hands and moved half of the ivy back to the wall. "Is to walk backward to the workbench and wait for me."

Evren remained silent, but he took a deep breath as the ivy around his body lessened. Relief smoothing the line between his brows.

"And my second option?" he asked, meeting her eyes. He didn't look well. Sweat had broken out across his forehead, his body trembling, but perhaps it was from the magick. Or from the weight of the ivy.

"Your second option," Tallulah said, pausing her hands to take a deep breath. "Your second option is to leave."

Evren's brows jumped to his hairline. His ruggedly handsome face softened as he weighed his options.

She moved her hands again. The rest of the ivy lifted, and now he was free. Free to leave. Free to take her to Valebridge and collect his coin. Free to kill her.

"Why would you let me go?" He took his time to sit up, but not any further than that. She stood above him, squaring her shoulders to make herself appear taller.

Be strong.

"Because I am making a choice," she said, annoyed. "I don't want to hurt you. But I also don't want you to hurt me. Take this as a truce. I'll spare your life right here and now, if you spare mine."

His gaze narrowed, sending a chill down Tallulah's spine.

Surely, this was a mistake. Spineless, childish, dreamer of a woman.

Slowly, he rose, his frame towering above hers. She inclined her head, keeping her hands ready in case he jumped toward her again. The shackles gleamed in the daylight, the sight of them making her stomach turn.

"You would let me go, knowing what I am," he whispered. Confusion and anger battled across his features.

"Yes," Tallulah replied, "but will you let *me* go knowing what *I* am." Her stomach was in knots as she waited. Her hands were nervous, but she kept them steady. She didn't want to hurt this man. She didn't want to hurt anyone. She just wanted to be left *alone*.

EVREN COULDN'T BELIEVE what this woman, this Enchantress, suggested. Would she really let him go after what he'd done to her? What he plans to do to the other Enchantresses he finds?

It must be a trap. There isn't any way she would simply let him live.

"I don't believe you," Evren said, taking a step backward. "The moment my back is turned, you'll kill me. You can try to seduce me with those unnatural, blue eyes woman but I've seen the destruction of your kind. Have learned firsthand just how vile you are."

The Enchantress's eyes widened, and she took a step back, putting even more distance between them.

"I. Don't. Trust. You," Evren clipped out, continuing to step backward until he pressed his back against the workbench.

She stood there, saying nothing but watching his every move. Her eyes filled again with tears and as they did, his stomach dropped. Why did he care if she cried?

"You're wrong," she whispered, still standing in the center of the domed room.

Evren glanced at her. She looked frail, but more so, she looked tired. He could try again to attack her, but it seemed to be no use. Her magick was fast, the ivy lethal. If he left now, would she kill him the moment turned his back? If she didn't, he could tell the others where she was. Bring more bodies, more men—

But did he want to?

He was tired too. Down to the very last inch of his soul. He was tired. The last year had taken so much from him and right now, the call to the drink was the only thing he could think about.

Maybe she'd kill him when he turned his back, maybe she'd kill him before he even stepped a foot into the snow. But he would try. Would try to leave her here, for now, if it meant heading straight back to the Blackwind Tavern and buying a half dozen pints. Anything to numb the pain in his leg. The pain in his heart for who he was. Who he used to be.

"Okay." Evren rolled his shoulders, his addiction deciding his fate for him. "I'll spare your life if you spare mine. Let me go and I'll let you be."

His head spun and doubt made his knees weak, but he was determined to get out of here. Determined to get back to Davenport and away from this Enchantress.

"And you won't tell anyone I'm here." She raised her hands slightly as if she readied herself to call upon the ivy. Her blue eyes were no longer lined with tears, but they shone brightly anyway. Maybe it was hope shining in them. Maybe it was fear.

"I'll tell no one." The lie felt thick in his throat, but he hadn't any choice. He needed to get out of here, and this was his way.

She's saving you, the little voice inside his head whispered. And maybe she was saving him, but it didn't change what she was. Didn't change the law.

Silence hung between them for several moments. The Enchantress in the middle of the greenhouse and Evren backed into a corner against the cedar workbench.

She took a step forward, her sage dress draping across the stone floor. "I'm going to unshackle you, and once I do, you will leave out the front door. You will leave and you will not come back."

Her eyes narrowed, the silver glint of the key catching his eye. He nodded and as he did, she took a step closer. Then another step, and another until she was mere inches away from him. Her face met his chest, and he had to dip his head low to meet her eyes.

He inhaled. She smelled of perfume, something floral and sweet he couldn't quite name. She kept her eyes on his face as she slid the key into the shackles. Heat bloomed against his skin as their hands brushed. He cleared his throat, not moving a muscle for fear of the ivy she'd call upon him. Once she slid the shackles off completely, he rubbed the soreness out of his wrists.

"Thank you," he said with a smile, before quickly wiping it away. She didn't return it, only stepping backward, giving him space.

"Go." She gestured to the door.

Evren wasn't sure why he hesitated. He still couldn't believe she'd let him go unharmed. But slowly his boots stepped forward, the scrape and scruff against the stone the only sound between them. Once he reached the door of the greenhouse, he peered behind him, expecting to see the Enchantress. But she wasn't there. So, he quietly slipped out the door and into the cold, bitter daylight.

A few miles back into the woods, Evren remembered the flask he'd stored in his pocket. Dropping to his knees, he stumbled to untwist the cap before swallowing the contents in a single gulp.

The shakiness he'd felt the past two days subsided, his head quieted, the ache in his leg soothed, and for a moment he didn't care about the Enchantress. Didn't care that he'd let her slip free, or rather, she let him. All he cared about was getting back to the tavern and chasing this feeling.

SEVEN

BIRDS CHIRPED THROUGH THE CRACKED WINDOW AS
Tallulah shoved her botany books and a few notebooks into her
small leather bag. It felt silly to pack these things in such a time
of haste, but she didn't care. She wanted them with her. The
notebooks alone would deem themselves useful if she ended up
in the forest.

She'd made good use of her time this last year, cataloging all
the different plants she encountered and grew. Shoving the last
notebook into her bag, she slouched on the sofa and did a final
look around.

The moment Evren stepped toward the doorway yesterday,
she'd known she would need to leave the greenhouse. Would
need to put as much distance as possible between herself and
Davenport. She didn't trust Evren for a second and was truly
shocked when he'd agreed to go. She'd waited up all night. Fear
that he'd return keeping her from sleep. But now that it was just
before dawn, she was ready to make her move.

With her bag packed and her boots laced, she peered out the
greenhouse door. The sun still slept, and darkness remained.
Though, even in the dimming moonlight, it was bright from

the freshly fallen snow. She tugged her cable-knit sweater closer to her body, wishing she'd had a cloak.

She didn't know where she headed. All she knew was she could no longer stay. A tear slipped from her eye, freezing upon her cheek in the chilly air. She would miss the greenhouse. Would miss her plants and flowers and the birds that regularly visited her.

But she turned anyway, heading for the clearing just beyond the edge of the forest. No homes, no villages or farms. Only the earth and the crashing waves of the sea. But she remembered an old fishing shanty. No one appeared to be maintaining it when she was there last Spring, and she certainly couldn't imagine anyone would be there in this weather. About an hour walk from her greenhouse, so she'd stop there to take a break from the freezing wind until the sun eventually rose.

As she trudged through the snow, her mind drifted to her life before King Roman's uprising. To the peace and love she felt tending to the royal gardens. To the warmth and affection she missed being surrounded by the other Enchantresses. They had become her family when her own dismissed her.

Quickly, her memories turned on her. Reminding her of the horrors the royal guards and hunters afflicted as King Roman declared magick illegal. Enchantresses were sworn to protect those in Teravie, and she knew in her heart that despite what Evren claimed last night, none of them would've hurt another person without cause.

Just as she decided she couldn't.

Wouldn't.

Tallulah wasn't sure why Evren's words affected her in the way they did. His opinion was not one she cared for, and yet as she pulled her frozen feet through the snow, it was all she could think of. The way he looked at her with such disgust. As if she were the monster in the room, not him.

Halfway to the cliffs, the sky shifted to purple; the sun

inching its way into the sky. The trees in the distance were faint, freshly covered in snow and, behind them, the small wooden fishing shanty. Relief spread through her shoulders and false heat bloomed in her chest, imagining the rest she could take once there. Her boots crunched upon the snow, the crashing of the waves soothing her soul.

"Well fancy that, we didn't even need to go looking for you."

Her heart stopped, her blue eyes stretching wide. The hunters approached swiftly. Tallulah's body clenched. The same two hunters she'd almost killed protecting that boy. They'd come back for her. Likely sensed her magick when she used it on Evren.

Dropping her bag, she lifted her wrists to call her magick again. The sound of the blood rushing in her ears drowning out the crashing waves.

Be strong.

A piercing pain sliced through her right shoulder, sending her backwards before she had the chance to summon the ivy. Her head smacked the frozen ground. She tried to sit up, tried to move, but was unable. The arrow had sliced the upper part of her arm as it passed by; the pain searing from the tip of her shoulder down to her toes. Hot tears burned bitter lines down her cheeks as her magick was silenced. The effects of the poison arrow coursed through her entire body.

The men approached—sour ale and smoke furled off them. They pulled her roughly to her feet.

"Did you think we wouldn't come back for you, Enchantress," one man snarled.

Tallulah gasped again as they shoved her forward, the throbbing in her arm weakening her knees. They pulled her forward again. Closer to the trees, closer to Davenport and away from the cliffs and the fishing shanty.

The men gripped her on either side, dragging her by her

elbows. She wanted to fight, but the pain in her arm and shoulder was debilitating and before she knew it, they clasped her wrists together. The dreadful sting of frost-bitten iron rubbed against her exposed skin.

Eight

THE THIRD PINT OF ALE WENT DOWN AS EASILY AS THE first. Evren sat in the same booth he and Markus had shared several nights ago, his mind racing and replaying his encounter with the Enchantress.

How had he gotten into such a predicament? And why had she let him go? He couldn't wrap his head around it.

He brought his fourth pint to his lips, taking a long pull of the bitter ale.

She'd let him go when his one job in the entire country was to capture her and sell her off to the king. His thoughts were at war with each other.

She should've killed me. But never did he think; *I should've killed her.*

But she didn't kill him.

She didn't even try. Every time Evren had found himself in an uncertain position, it was out of defense because *he* attacked *her.* She had pulled him in from the cold, tended to the wound on the back of his head. She'd fed him and didn't even poison him.

He couldn't come to terms with her generosity. Nothing was ever free, so why spare his life when he hadn't given hers a second thought? It ate away at him. Every second since he left the greenhouse, this Enchantresses filled his mind with poisonous thoughts.

Maybe they're not all bad.

Maybe it's us who should be locked away.

Even if he hadn't planned to kill her, he knew what taking her to King Roman meant. Knew he'd drain every last bit of her magick until she was nothing but a corpse.

He shuddered and doing so surprised him. He had captured and turned in six Enchantresses yet this one left him questioning everything.

THE NEXT MORNING began just the way most of Evren's morning began. With a headache. He rubbed at his eyes before peering out of the dusty curtains of his room at the inn. Nearly dawn. The tavern wouldn't open for several hours, so he'd have to keep himself busy until then.

Outside, more snow had fallen, leaving a blanket of white across the port city. Large ships docked at the harbor, their sailors still aboard, likely dreaming of calm seas and wild women. The snowstorm quickly approaching had stalled their departure. Evren smiled then, thinking of how close he was to boarding one of those ships himself. He decided this morning as he clasped his cloak, he would not leave Davenport until the deed was done.

He just needed one more Enchantress.

He just needed *her*.

His boots turned toward the forest, pulling him in the same direction he'd found those hunters. The same direction he'd found Tallu—no, he wouldn't let himself get familiar. She was his bounty, and he would bring her in for his prize.

She spared your life, that poisonous little voice whispered.

Oh, how he hated that little voice. Always chiming in when it had no business to. Even if it was right. Maybe she spared his life, but he had a duty to uphold. He swore an oath to his king and to his king, he would stay true.

He dodged his way around heavy limbs of pine and evergreen. His headache had lessened, likely due to the frigid air now filling his lungs.

A welcome distraction.

His mind drifted back to the Blackwind Tavern. Back to another pint. As it always did. To another glass of the numbing liquid he'd become too reliant on this last year. He'd never been a drinker, not when he was a boy and certainly not in the royal guard. But something about how it soothed his restless hands and wandering thoughts after his injury was all-consuming. And not easily forgotten or ignored.

He stopped, his boots skidding in the snow. He was almost to the cliffs and just beyond it would be the clearing where he'd make his way to the greenhouse. But the undeniable force drawing him back to the tavern pulled harder than any promise of coin could. The ale wasn't a want; it was a need. A need that he knew, if left unattended, would swallow him whole.

He closed his eyes and took a deep breath, cursing himself for not remembering to fill his flask before he left. The air froze in his lungs just as the snow had frozen his toes. He stood there, eyes closed and saw the coin promised by King Roman slip through his fingers as he abandoned his mission for a glass of ale. It would be too easy to let her win. But deep down, he knew who the real enemy was.

The ale.

Anger replaced the ice in his chest. Hot and quick. Then he saw the Enchantress behind his eyes perched in her greenhouse. Her long, dark hair. Her tanned skin and cerulean eyes. His eyes snapped open, and fury guided his next steps. He would not let the drink take his victory. And he would *certainly* not let this Enchantress get away.

Evren made the final descent out of the woods and toward the cliffs. Muffled voices carried through the wind. .

"Did you think we wouldn't come back for you, Enchantress?"

Evren knew that voice. His pace quickened and soon enough, he was face to face with the two hunters he'd dragged back to Davenport the day he met the Enchantress. And behind them on the ground, there she was. Red coated the snow. A bloodied arrow sat several feet behind the Enchantress, lodged in the ground like a tether of death. His heart slammed, pushing against his ribcage.

"Captain Fletcher," Jasper said with widened eyes, stepping forward with a salute.

"What is going on here?" Evren asked.

It was then the Enchantress lifted her head, her eyes wide with thick silver tears streaming down her cheeks. They had gagged her mouth with a cloth, her wrists rubbed raw from the freezing temperature and the bite of iron. Her shoulder...

"I asked you a question," Evren snarled. The men straightened, snow collecting atop their blue cloaks.

"We were just bringing her into Davenport," Alexander said, his blonde beard tickled white from the heavily falling flakes. "Just doing our job, sir."

The condescending tone lit a flame of annoyance in Evren that he couldn't ignore.

"And the arrow?" Evren avoided the woman's gaze. He didn't know why, but he couldn't face her this way. He may hunt Enchantresses, but seeing her defenseless and bloodied in the snow didn't sit right with him. Not after the kindness she'd shown him.

Not after she let you live.

"She raised her hands." Jasper turned to the Enchantress and kicked snow at her face.

She winced before slamming her eyes shut.

"We had to take her down before she used her magick on us." Jasper spat. Evren followed the trail of saliva. His eyes widened. She recoiled back, trying to turn her head, but she wasn't quick enough. It landed right on her cheek, just below her eye. "Think you could best us you little who—"

"*Enough*." Evren stepped towards the men. "You are enlisted by King Roman to bring these women in unharmed. What do you think unharmed *means*, gentlemen?" He gestured to the Enchantress' shoulder. To the red in the snow that matched the red covering her sweater.

She furrowed her dark brows when she caught his eye, and for whatever reason, he knew what he had to do.

"The rule is clear, sir," Alexander stated, "if an Enchantress raises her hands to you then—"

"You are relieved of your duties." Evren squared his shoulders. "You are to return your badges at once. Look for Lieutenant Benedict at the Blackwind Tavern, he's my second in command."

The men shook their heads, disbelief clear in their eyes but neither of them moved.

"If I find out the two of you didn't turn in your badges, there will be hell to pay."

"But sir—" Jasper stepped forward, his fiery hair glowing in the snow lit light.

"That was an order." Evren's fingers tapped on his leg in a furious rhythm. Not to mention, if the witch lost any more blood, he wouldn't be able to trade her for his coin and, by the looks of the snow, she was losing it quickly. "You've proven to me you can't complete a simple task. I'll deliver her to King Roman *myself*, without further damage."

The men's faces reddened, and they gaped like fish. Their argument was clearly not over.

"Go," he said, firm and direct.

The men eyed him for a moment. A few profanities were muffled under their breaths before they started forward.

As Jasper walked by, Evren stuck out his arm, slamming it into his chest and stopping him short.

"The key." Evren kept his eyes on the Enchantress.

She watched, no longer crying, her eyes wide and questioning. Her brows had softened, but her face had gone as pale as the snow.

The hunter dug into his pants pocket and fished out the tiny silver key that would unlock the Enchantress from her shackles. Snatching it, Evren quickly placed it in his pocket for good keeping.

"Now leave," he said, and the men, this time, didn't question him as they turned and disappeared back into the forest.

NINE

EVERYTHING IN TALLULAH'S BODY WAS ON FIRE. FROM her arm where the arrow struck her, to the tips of her toes, frozen in her boots. She thought for certain she'd met her demise when the poisonous arrow hit her. Thought her fate had been decided the moment the iron shackles sealed around her wrists.

But then there he was.

Evren had come back, and from the repugnance on his face, he'd come back to do just as the men he sent away intended to do. Take her to Valebridge and trade her life, her soul, for a bit of coin.

But why bother sending the men away at all? Why not let them finish the job? Unless he was desperate for the coin.

Yes. He must be a desperate man, indeed.

"Can you walk?" Evren peered down at her where she still kneeled in the snow.

Tallulah wasn't certain if she *could* walk with the amount of pain she was in and refused to look down at the crimson snow. The air was rich with iron, making her stomach queasy. But she certainly wouldn't give him the satisfaction of dragging her. She rose to her feet, inch by excruciating inch, until her chin was level with his chest. As she did, he gently untied the cloth from her mouth. She stretched her jaw, the pain there nothing compared to her arm.

"Yes." She glared at him, her nostrils flaring from the scent of the blood and the unsettled anger in her chest. She bit down on her tongue to distract herself. Her arm felt heavy and useless, her body frozen, and her hopes of escaping diminished.

Evren just watched her. His green eyes snagged on the wound on her shoulder. White flecks of snow littered his dark auburn hair and while she expected him to be just as forceful as the other men had been, his distance surprised her.

"Let's go." A certain softness in his words caught Tallulah off guard. He'd been so straightforward and blunt when they'd spoken last. But this was different. As if he cared. As if he sought her for a different reason...

"Are you taking me to Valebridge?" Tallulah asked through a wince, but the effort to speak was too much. Her body crumpled forward; her hands unable to break her fall.

Evren's hands were there before she could register what happened. Gripping her forearms, steadying her. She kept her eyes to the ground, confused by his touch. By his tenderness.

"Not today," he whispered in her ear.

For a moment, relief replaced the pain. For a moment, hope ignited again and at that, she dared to look him in the eyes. "Take us back to the greenhouse so I can tend to your wound," Evren whispered. "The king won't be happy with a damaged product, and I intend to get every last coin he's offering."

Tallulah's heart sank with every word. Every syllable. The flame of hope doused. It shouldn't surprise her to hear it. He was a hunter, and she was the prey. But it stung anyway, just as much as the iron around her wrists. As much as the poison dripping into her veins. She had spared his life, and he was more than willing to toss hers aside for a bit of gold.

She didn't speak during their trek back to the greenhouse.

This was how it was always going to end, anyway. *At least*

you made it a year. And she had. She'd made it a year into her freedom before it would be stripped away. And that, at least, was something.

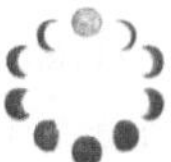

DESPITE THE LOOMING hunter behind her, Tallulah sighed as she landed on the old sofa inside the greenhouse. She took a deep inhale. Jasmine and mint and thyme all greeted her, and she savored it.

A throat cleared to her right, interrupting her quick moment of solitude.

"I need to look at your arm." Evren leaned against the glass wall with his arms crossed.

Tallulah simply nodded. What other choice did she have? He stepped forward, but then paused, his hands fidgeting at his sides. Was he nervous?

"I won't bite." Tallulah laughed, which quickly turned to a cry as the pain in her shoulder flowed clear down her arm.

In an instant, Evren was there again. Kneeling in front of her like she was a Mother-damned queen. Like he wasn't about to fix her up to sell her off. She hadn't even heard him move. But his hands went instinctually to her arm, pressing against the wound. She was so shocked by his touch it took her a moment to realize the pain had lessened from the pressure.

Evren cleared his throat again. "Do you have...a thread and needle? I'll need to stitch it."

His face was only inches away from hers. After-shave and freshly fallen snow replaced the herbs lingering in the space. If she turned, even in the slightest, her lips would brush against the dark red scruff on his jaw. So, she sat perfectly still. Swallowing thickly and focusing on her breathing.

"In the second drawer." She nodded to the rickety chest of drawers sitting in the corner.

Evren stood quickly and headed for the chest.

"There's a needle and thread," Tallulah continued, "but you'll also need to apply some yarrow."

Evren spun on his heels, his brows arched in confusion.

Tallulah stifled a laugh. "Just because you're hauling me away to Valebridge doesn't mean I should sit and suffer while you do so. I imagine I'll do plenty of that when I'm there." Her voice broke on the last part and for a moment she swore she saw Evren flinch. "The yarrow will help ease the pain and fight off infection."

"I..." Evren reached up to scratch the back of his head. His eyes were wide as he glanced around the abundance of different foliage taking over the greenhouse. "I don't know what—"

"Don't worry." Her breaths came in short pants, her chest constricting with each one. "I'll show you."

And then the room spun, and her vision went dark.

Ten

Evren knew they couldn't stay here long.
Markus expected him in the next week and he had a job to do.
But as soon as the woman's head hit the sofa, he had no intention of leaving. His wounded leg was piercing, and his body
ached for ale, but he couldn't leave her here.

I need to make my coin.

Yes, that was the only reason he stayed. To stitch her up and
bring her to King Roman in one piece. It most definitely wasn't
because of the hurt look in her blue eyes, or the electric pulse he
felt kneeling beside her, or that she spared his life on more than
one occasion.

No.

She was the means to end his current situation, and that was
all.

He grabbed the thread and needle from the drawer and
hurried back to the sofa where the Enchantress lay unconscious.
Her body was freezing, yet clammy. Fever and infection would
take her before the blood loss would, but he was still determined to suture her to the best of his abilities.

He readied the needle and took a deep breath. Exhaling
through his lips, he was grateful she was unconscious for what

came next. Even though he would sell her off to the corrupt king, he didn't like to hurt anyone. Even in times such as this.

You're not any better. He dismissed that little voice in his head. He needed to focus.

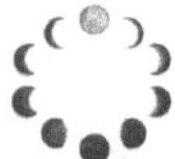

THE ENCHANTRESS SLEPT for several hours, the wound on her shoulder stitched nicely together, but without the plants she'd suggested, infection was at risk of taking over.

Evren stood perplexed, staring at the rows and rows of different plants. In some ways, they all looked the same. But they were all so completely different.

She let out a whimpered, broken cry and it had Evren snapping his head toward her. Sweat coated her forehead and upper lip. Her wound had swollen and angry red bubbles came to the surface. She was running out of time.

His fists clenched as his heart constricted. He could easily leave. Get the drink his body desperately screamed for. Then, head straight to the Jade Guild and meet with his uncle. Ask him for the last bit of coin he needed to catch a ship—

Evren's fists clenched at his sides. He'd do just about anything other than ask for his uncle's help. He needed to do this. Heal the Enchantress, take her to Valebridge, get the hell out of this country.

He let out a terse breath and gripped the ends of his hair. Then, his eyes snagged on a small wooden box buried under a heap of ivy atop the workbench. He brushed the vines aside, careful not to push too hard in case they pushed back. He wasn't sure he'd ever be able to look at the plant the same way again. Shuddering, he refocused on the box. "For Emergencies" was labeled across the top in flowing soft cursive.

He glanced at the Enchantress, still unconscious on the sofa. Something stirred in his chest, but Evren ignored it.

Carefully, he opened the box and pulled out a dried, yellowing bundle of herbs. He had no idea if this was the yarrow the Enchantress spoke of, but he didn't have much time to ponder it.

He let his instincts guide him next, finding a mortar and pestle, grinding the dried plant to dust. Evren added a bit of now thawed water from the rain bucket to form a thick paste. Once he was satisfied, or at least thought there was nothing else he could do, he took the mortar full of paste to her side.

Kneeling again, he set the bowl down. The silver key in his pocket felt like a lead weight. Pulling him down with each moment he left her shackled.

Her brows pinched together, and her eyelids twitched. She was unsettled. In pain.

Evren couldn't explain why, but his thumb grazed her brow, smoothing it out. She relaxed, her features softening against his touch. Quickly, he drew his hand away. He wouldn't get distracted. He had a job to do.

Ignoring the hammering in his heart, he decided that in her current condition she wasn't a threat. So, going against every instinct, he pulled the key from his pocket, watched as it slipped into the lock, felt his fingers twist until the iron fell to the floor with a loud crash. Then, before he could think any further, he scooped up the thick salve he'd made and applied it directly to the wound.

He had never once believed in Mother Gaia, or any other deity for that matter. But his next words whispered were a plea to anyone that would hear them.

"Please be okay."

Sun filtered through the domed ceiling of the greenhouse, sweeping away the brutality of the night prior. Tallulah fought against waking, but the dryness of her mouth forced her to sit. She braced herself, waiting to feel the excruciating pain from her wound, but all she felt was a bit of a sting. Her wrists ached more than her arm, red angry lines marked her skin. But despite it, her breath came easier.

Her wrists were free.

Sliding her feet to the floor, she gasped as they landed not on the icy ground she was expecting but upon Evren. She tucked her feet back under herself, hoping she didn't wake him.

His body sprawled across the stone ground next to the sofa. Her heart flipped, thinking he may jump up at any moment and relock that cursed iron around her wrists. But he didn't. He simply rolled, rubbing at his eyes and the sleep that still lined them.

"I'm sorry," Tallulah whispered.

Evren rolled himself up and smiled, softly. Her stomach dropped. Though the weary look on his face told Tallulah he wasn't exactly pleased to be sleeping on the floor next to her, so she brushed the feeling aside.

"How's your arm?" he asked, his voice flat.

He scratched a hand down his stubbled jaw, and she studied him for a moment, unsure what he was getting at. Not sure why, exactly, they were back here.

"Better than yesterday, but still painful," she said. She kept her body still, not wanting to risk him realizing he had left her unshackled. "Why are you—"

"So—"

Tallulah bit her lip as they spoke in unison.

"You first." She gestured for him to continue. Not missing the way his eyes immediately went to her hands as she did so.

He stood, his frame blocked the sun momentarily as he towered over her. Tallulah had forgotten just how tall he was. She swallowed.

"So," he started again, "the yarrow really works." He

pointed to her arm before taking a few steps backward, leaning against the greenhouse wall.

"It does." Tallulah ran her hand over her shoulder, careful not to touch the stitches. Still sore and healing, but the pain was more manageable. It was only a temporary fix—the yarrow would wear and the true agony that hid underneath would come crashing back.

She was grateful he found it. Grateful he'd taken the time to consider her pain.

The silence that filled between them was awkward and heavy. Tallulah's stomach rumbled, but she still did not move.

Evren avoided her eyes, focusing instead on any other thing. The room was bright despite it being the middle of Winter, the white light of the sun drenched each of her plants and flowers. On a normal morning, Tallulah would love this moment. The sun dripping in, the plants reaching their limbs for any bit of warmth. But this morning, her stomach curdled as she sat in her favorite spot.

"Evren," she said, feeling bold and rather quite tired of sitting in silence. He turned to her but said nothing. "Are you taking me to Valebridge today?"

She didn't want to know the answer, but she had to ask the question. She was in good enough shape to sit on a horse. Decent enough to be presented to the king. And with her magick still nulled from the poison, it'd be wise of him to take her now.

Her heart slammed against her chest, but it was her traitorous stomach that flipped as Evren's green eyes met hers.

"Not today, Enchantress."

Eleven

Markus took a final drag from his cigar before quickly stamping it into the glass ashtray. He'd been in Copenspire for a week and was nowhere near finding an Enchantress. There was no point in being defeated, because once Evren joined him, he had no doubts they'd have better luck together.

His fingers drummed on the table. He was impatient for him to arrive; their meeting spot determined before they'd parted ways back in Davenport. Though, to his annoyance, they never set a time. So he was left waiting around the decrepit seaside town with nothing to do but piss some of his coin away on a game or two of poker.

He sat as a bystander tonight though, not willing to chance losing any more of his shillings in case that dark-haired, smart mouthed arse came back. The man had played Markus like a fool last night, raising bet after bet just to win on a bluff. After he left, the barkeep had told him he was a usual out of towner who makes his rounds to poker games around the coast.

Markus shook his head, frustrated at the coin he lost before taking a sip of his stale ale. Evren would've laughed in his face for being so reckless with his money.

The hours ticked by and day turned to dusk and still there

was no Evren in sight. Exhausted, and a bit irritated, he paid his tab and left to retire at the Swede Haven Inn.

"Sir." A man stepped into his path. Markus was too tired to remember his name, but knew his face from initiation a few nights ago in Davenport.

"What is it?" Markus continued his walk to the inn across the snowy cobbled street.

"It's Jasper and Alexander," the recruit said, the panic laced in his tone caused Markus to halt his steps. "They've been instructed to report to you by Lieutenant Benedict."

"And what is the cause for this?" Markus spun, shoving his hands in his pockets as the man fidgeted before him. "Evren is in charge of the recruits, not me."

The man before him looked at his boots, his hands twiddling at his sides. Man was generous, he truly looked no older than sixteen years. *Joseph*! Markus nearly snapped his fingers, finally remembering the boy's name from his initiation back in Davenport.

"Apparently Captain Fletcher has let Jasper and Alexander go off their duties, sir, and so Lieutenant Benedict sent them here to find you. See if you had any ideas why Captain Fletcher would do such a thing." Joseph fiddled with his cloak before finally tucking his hands behind his back.

Markus crossed his arms, nodding for the boy to continue.

He looked nervous as he swallowed. "According to Jasper and Alexander, Captain Fletcher took over their hunt. Stole an Enchantress right from out of their hands. Said he'd handle it himself, then dismissed them and told them to seek the Lieutenant. No one has seen or heard from him since."

Markus shook his head, a muscle in his jaw flexing. He'd never known Evren to break the rules, and stealing a hunt was certainly a *very* important rule not to break. Surely there was more to the story.

"Where are they?" Markus flexed his fingers. The tips of them numb from the frigid temperatures.

"They've just settled at the inn," Joseph gestured to the building to Markus' back.

Perfect. Markus spun without another word to the recruit.

THE SWEDE HAVEN Inn was quaint and despite Copenspire being a shite-hole, it provided decent beds and meals. The two men Evren had apparently dismissed waited in the foyer. Their surly looks and nearly frost-bitten fingers a sign their journey from Davenport was unkind.

"In the dining hall," Markus said as he passed the men by.

He wasn't used to being so harsh with his tone, but if Evren taught him anything, it was to lead by authority. Make sure the men knew who was in charge from the moment he walked into the room. So that's what Markus would do.

The men followed him into the dining hall, where the three of them took seats around a large wooden table. Floorboards creaked beneath their wet boots, the heavy floral drapes keeping the heat from escaping through the thin windows. The dim lanterns kept much to the imagination. The silence unnerved him, save for the occasional sweeping of a broom from the women cleaning after dinner service.

"Explain yourselves." Markus reclined back in his chair.

The men eyed each other for a moment. Alexander's blonde beard still housed flecks of ice and snow from their travels. He glanced at Jasper, whose red hair stuck out like a flame in the lantern light.

"Captain Fletcher was out of line—"

"That wasn't what I asked," Markus leaned forward, placing his elbows on the table. *Command the room.* Coming to Evren's immediate defense was second nature. They'd been best friends all their lives. Surely, if he dismissed these men, it was for a valid reason. "I said, explain *yourselves*. Why were you dismissed?"

After what felt like ages, the men told their story and Markus was exhausted. From what it sounded like, Evren had no right to dismiss the men. They'd simply defended themselves against the Enchantress who threatened to use magick against them.

Despicable woman.

No matter the reason, Markus decided as he collapsed onto his bed at the inn, that if Evren didn't show himself in the next week, he'd return to Davenport and figure this out for himself.

TWELVE

"You're doing it wrong," Tallulah said through a laugh.

Evren threw the watering can back onto the workbench before spinning to her. It landed with a loud bang that made Tallulah jump. Her pulse stammered, and she took a steadying breath.

"How can I possibly water a plant incorrectly?" Evren's freckled forehead broke out in a sheen of sweat.

Tallulah laughed again. She enjoyed watching him struggle.

"By all means,"—he crossed his arms like a child—"do it yourself."

This only made Tallulah laugh harder. She'd felt much better the last few days. The constant care from Evren combined with the mix of yarrow had given her shoulder more movement, but still not enough to tend to her daily chores on her own. The yarrow was running low, so she needed to save her energy, for what, she didn't know. Evren, despite the constant furrowed brows, had been almost enjoyable to be around.

Almost.

"I would do it myself." Tallulah straightened herself up on the sofa. "But if you've forgotten, my arm is still on the mend."

Evren sighed, his face softening for a moment. Was it guilt that hung in his forest eyes?

Tallulah brushed it off, her eyes drifting to his hands where they hung at his sides. It wasn't the first time she'd noticed their tremble. Not to mention the restlessness and limp he walked with. She didn't remember it before, but now, she saw how desperately he tried to hide it.

"Now," Tallulah continued, pocketing the curiosities of his mannerisms for later, "the pothos must be watered weekly but the spider plants there"—she pointed to a group of rather full green spindly plants hanging in the corner—"needs to be watered monthly. And today is that day."

She didn't miss the way Evren's eyes rolled, but he still gathered the small metal watering can back from where he'd tossed it and took her instructions in silence.

It seemed silly to keep up with her plants when she knew Evren's goal was to bring her to the king. But she'd asked him yesterday and the day prior if he'd take her to Valebridge. To which he replied softly, *"Not today, Enchantress."*

It would be absurd for her to question why not, but still, it tickled at the back of her mind like a scratch just out of reach. Why were they still here? Surely, she was healed enough to deem fit for magick harvesting. But she didn't voice her concerns; she wasn't that stupid.

Evren watered the last of the plants, a task that took nearly the whole afternoon. When he finished, he slumped on the sofa next to Tallulah, an act so casual she almost forgot who he was.

What he was.

"Why bother with so many damn plants?" He ran an unsteady hand down his face.

She watched him out of the corner of her eye. If she turned her head to face him, their faces would be close. Too close. So instead, she kept herself pointed forward. Ignoring the pounding in her chest and the scent of soil and pine wafting off him. She kept herself facing the back of the greenhouse, where she surely wouldn't find her stomach faltering at anyone's eyes.

"Because they bring me joy," she finally answered. And it was true. While creating plants from her magick brought her the *most* joy, planting the foliage over the last year just as a human would keep her busy. It brought her a sense of purpose and accomplishment.

Her skin raised, the hairs on her neck prickling. She turned then to find Evren watching her, a smile dancing on his lips.

He cleared his throat, his face returning to its typical stern demeanor. Did he look more pale than usual?

"Seems a bit odd, that's all," he said. "Why have so many plants if you can't even eat any of them?"

Tallulah tipped her head back again, her long dark hair dancing down her shoulders and over her arms and laughed. She'd never thought about that.

"Fair point." She shot Evren a smile. Her stomach flipped as he returned her smile with one of his own. A rarity. An achievement.

"I'm going to wash up, then I'll see what I can find for dinner."

He stood from the sofa and made his way to the door that led to the small room that housed her water barrels.

"Lucky you," she said sarcastically. "I haven't had a proper bath since—"

She bit her lip and glanced at Evren, who propped himself against the doorway, arms crossed, as they so often were.

"I'm sorry about that." His gaze redirected to her shoulder.

Her stomach erupted with a fluttering sensation. It was the first time he'd apologized for anything and it made her feel...it made her feel everything.

"It's okay," she said with a shrug. "This wasn't your fault."

Evren nodded, a look of uncertainty passing over his face. Maybe, in a way, the damage to her shoulder was his fault. If he hadn't found her, hadn't tried to take her, maybe none of this would've happened. But before she could reassure him, he turned. Tallulah resettled on the sofa.

"I could help you," he whispered from the doorway, startling her. "If you wanted, I mean…I understand if not, but if you just wanted some help I could—"

He let out a long breath.

Tallulah couldn't help the smile that twitched at her lips. It wasn't often he stumbled over his words, and something about him doing it now made her heart warm.

"Okay," she said.

Evren's head snapped up, his green eyes meeting hers.

"Okay?" he asked and when she nodded, he met her back at the sofa, reaching for her hand.

"Okay, hunter."

Heating the water for the basin took ages, giving Tallulah several extra moments to reconsider what she was about to do. Before she could protest and change her mind, Evren popped his head out of the bathing room.

"Ready?"

Swallowing, she nodded before joining him in the room. She wouldn't undress, she couldn't imagine doing so. Instead, she sat on the floor, resting her head backward so her long hair draped over the side of the tub, the ends dipping into the water. She closed her eyes, focusing on her breathing.

He will not kill you, Tallulah. He needs you alive.

A weak attempt to settle her nerves, but it was all she had.

Water trickled down her hair as Evren poured from a pitcher. Over and over, he dipped it into the water and ran it over her hair with such gentleness. She kept her eyes pressed tight as his fingers massaged into her scalp, the scent of jasmine from her homemade soap calming her nerves even further. Her spine tickled as his fingers graced her bare nape and before she could let out her next breath, the water trickled over her scalp again.

"Better?" Evren asked.

Tallulah opened her eyes. He was kneeling beside her, his shirt damp from leaning over the tub to fill the pitcher. His freckled cheeks were flushed and, despite the fluttering in her stomach earlier, she smiled.

"Evren," she whispered, keeping her eyes locked on his. "Are you taking me to Valebridge today?"

Her hands restlessly picked at each other in her lap. Every time she asked, she feared the answer. She knew one day he would say yes. But it couldn't be today, could it? Not when he agreed to water her hundreds of plants, and not when he smiled and laughed with her. Not when he'd washed her hair with such gentleness.

Dread pooled in her gut as she watched him. Watched and waited for her fate to be determined.

"Not today, Enchantress." He pulled her to her feet and handed her a cloth for her hair. He did not return her smile. Did not offer anything else before he turned and left her alone.

Not today.

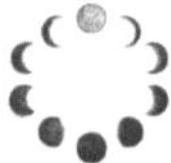

THE ROOM HAD DARKENED except for the light of the moon through the domed roof. Evren laid on the floor in the same spot as he had the past several nights while the Enchantress peacefully slept on the sofa.

As much as he hated to admit it, her presence was a comfort and a welcome distraction to the treachery brought down on him with no drink. It'd been five long days, and he felt every one of them. It was in his head; swimming with anxious thoughts. In his hands; they trembled and shook against his will. In his restlessness, his body could not understand the need for sleep when the need for ale was much stronger. All consuming to the point of insanity.

And he swore he would have already plummeted to those

dark depths of madness if it hadn't been for her. He chalked it up to needing to get her healthy for King Roman. That's all this was.

He glanced up at the Enchantress sleeping soundly on the sofa. Her lips pouted as if her dreams were unsatisfactory.

Probably not many happy moments to be thinking of.

Many times, he'd considered leaving to seek Davenport. It was on his mind even now as he laid awake on the stone ground. But whenever he'd put one foot toward the door, the Enchantress would invite him to join her on the sofa for a round of stories and his mind would shift back. She'd laugh and his heart would squeeze. She'd look at him and all thoughts of leaving would vanish. She'd trusted him today in a very real and vulnerable way.

That made him hate himself further.

She'd trusted him to help her, and it was a trust he didn't deserve nor one he could reciprocate.

He sighed and rubbed his hand through his hair. He had an oath to uphold and no reason to still be here. No reason he couldn't take her to Valebridge and acquire the bounty he sought.

The rational part of his mind screamed at him to leave with her now, collect his coin, and go. But something else stirred in him he didn't recognize. Something deep and foreign.

He replayed the feeling of his hands in her hair. The fire that erupted on his fingertips as they grazed her neck. He replayed those moments over and over until they made him question his entire being.

Rolling over, he faced away from the Enchantress. He needed to clear his head.

Though, despite it all, his gut had already decided her fate for him. He wouldn't leave her here unguarded, and he wouldn't take her to King Roman. At least not yet. Not until he figured out what this feeling was. What it could mean.

He was powerless in this situation, and he hated it because

whatever part of him that stirred restlessly, he was beginning to think only she could control it.

Thirteen

"Just try again," Evren pleaded. It'd been Tallulah's third attempt, and she still struggled to stretch her arm fully. "You have to begin moving it or it won't heal properly. If you keep coddling—"

"I'm not coddling it," Tallulah snapped, sinking back into the sofa. She ran a hand down her face, partially out of frustration and partially to conceal the tears.

She wiped a rogue tear away, and Evren's face fell.

She *was* coddling her arm. She wasn't sure if it was because it hurt or because she knew that once it healed, he'd send her to Valebridge. To her fate. Her death.

"All right." Evren sighed and took a step backward, then sipped from one of Tallulah's mugs—light blue with a gold filigree handle. It was one of her favorites; the light blue reminding her of a cloudless day. She'd found it in the greenhouse and had used it nearly every day since. When Evren chose it this morning for the pine needle tea she'd made them, it warmed her much like the tea itself.

She shivered, running her hands down her arms. The snow hadn't let up all day and tonight would be the coldest of Winter yet. Another storm had begun, there was no denying that.

"If you don't want to keep trying, that's fine. All I'm saying is by keeping your arm locked in one position like that, you're more likely to be sore." He watched her cautiously over his mug.

Tallulah averted her eyes, not wanting to get lost in his like she foolishly had a few days ago when they'd been laughing over the plants.

"Fine," she said, closing her eyes and breathing deeply. She cracked one eye open when she heard Evren shuffle toward the sofa. He sank down next to her, leaving his mug of tea steaming on the workbench.

"Let me help," he said.

Her eyes shot open completely as her head snapped toward him. He looked genuine enough. His eyes had softened the last few days, even if he still had a nervous twitch about him. How is it that a line of sweat was always just above his brow when it was freezing cold in here?

Tallulah looked away again, not realizing how long she'd been staring. Before her cheeks could heat, she disregarded the interaction and sat straight.

"I don't need your help." She straightened her arm to stretch it fully. Pain shot through her elbow and cleared up to her shoulder. Wincing, she pulled her arm back close to her chest, exactly where she'd kept it since her injury. She had made a point since he washed her hair nearly a week ago that she simply could not ask for his help again. It was too vulnerable. Too weak.

Be strong.

"Go slower." Evren scooted closer. "Like this."

Gently, his fingers gripped her forearm. The heat of his touch seared through her ivory sweater, but she held her wits about her. Giving him the silent approval he sought. His fingers widened their grip around her arm, and he slowly straightened it for her.

The pain shot back through her elbow, but this time, the

intensity was less. More bearable. Further and further, he stretched her arm, his fingers delicate yet firm, until it was completely straight in front of her.

"How is the pain now?" Evren asked, his hand still upon her arm.

"It's okay," Tallulah whispered. Her heart slamming against her chest was more painful than her arm. Her memories reminded her of how his hands felt in her hair, on her skin.

"Okay." Evren dropped his hand and placed both of them in his lap. "We'll keep working on it, a few more days, and I'm sure the pain will cease completely. You'll be good as new."

He smiled, his eyes crinkling slightly at the corners, the freckles across his cheeks spreading. Perhaps his comment should ease her somehow. Reassure her that her arm wasn't a total waste. But all it did was remind her they were not friends, and that she was to be his prisoner.

Her magick was still silent, the poison from the arrow snuffing it out. She imagined it'd be several more weeks before she regained any control. And Evren knew it. She was defenseless. Was this his plan? To get her to trust him so she'd be more compliant to leave?

Her body stiffened at his closeness. At his eyes watching her. At his hand, still so close to her body.

Evren scooted just a bit further away, as if sensing her discomfort. "What is it? Have we pushed it too far?"

His brows creased and Tallulah hadn't the slightest clue why. Was he jesting with her?

"Enough games." She stood abruptly from the sofa.

"Games?" Evren recoiled back before standing from the sofa as well.

"Yes." She backed up until her body hit the workbench. "Enough with the niceties. You and I are not *friends*, Evren. Stop acting like it."

Confusion contorted his face as he retook his seat on the sofa.

"If you're to take me to Valebridge as your prisoner, just get it over with. Just please, stop this act." She wished she could use her magick right now. She would tie him up again with ivy and leave him for the snow to claim.

But deep down, she knew she didn't want that. She didn't want to hurt him. She certainly didn't want him to die. But what was it she wanted?

Almost two weeks trapped here with this hunter proved more confusing than anything she'd ever experienced. Surely, if there wasn't a handsome bounty tied to her head, Evren would've killed her already.

He watched her intently, the crease between his brows lessening and the brightness of his green eyes returning. But still, he said nothing.

Tallulah tapped her foot, the quiet bringing forth her anxiousness.

"So?" She crossed her arms. "Are you taking me to Valebridge today?"

At that, Evren stood and took a step forward. Then another. And another until he was right in front of her. She'd bury her face in his chest if he stepped any closer, so she tilted her head upwards to meet his face.

He stretched his hand, brushing lightly against hers.

"Not today, Enchantress."

She sucked in a sharp breath at the contact, but before she could say anything more, he turned away and left.

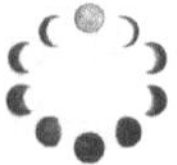

EVREN WAS ABSOLUTELY WASTING time and he knew it. He also knew the Enchantress would get her magick back any week now. The poison from the arrow would wear and, with her magick back, he didn't stand a chance against her if she tried anything.

And she would use it against him the first moment she could. Wouldn't she?

He wouldn't blame her if she did. Wouldn't fight her. He deserved it for what he'd done to the six Enchantresses before her. For what he planned to do with her. What was he doing here? Why was he stalling? He knew damn well she was in good enough shape for King Roman, so *why* was he still here?

"You're helpless." He slouched down, planting himself firmly against the outer wall of the greenhouse. The air stung his cheeks and bit the top of his ears. He shouldn't stay out long.

He glanced around the darkness as the snow blew in each direction in thick flurries. Clouds covered the sky, dark and looming.

He needed to go back inside, but his feet remained planted in the snow and ice. He couldn't go in. Because she was there. With her long dark hair and her smooth skin. With her laugh that sparked a flame within him, making him reconsider everything he'd done the last year. Then there was the matter of her eyes. The ones that saw too much. The eyes that danced behind his own each night when he went to sleep.

As much as he dreaded going back inside, he wasn't *so* much of an idiot to risk freezing to death. The snow had increased, and he could barely make out a foot in front of him. So, reluctantly, he pulled himself from the bitter ground and went in.

There wasn't much warmth inside the greenhouse, but it sure as hell beat staying outside during a snowstorm. A few candles remained lit in the main room, casting leafy shadows over the back wall.

He kicked off his boots, leaving them to dry by the front door. As if this were his home. As if he belonged here. Taking long, deliberate steps, he made his way down the tiny entryway. He wouldn't want to wake her if she'd already fallen asleep, so he kept his toes light. He hesitated as he got to the main room.

The Enchantress glanced at him before returning her attention to her book. "Are you just going to stand there?"

He'd only known the Enchantress a couple weeks now but he knew her well enough that the tone she used meant she wasn't pleased. Maybe she was frustrated at him still being here. Hell, he was frustrated with himself for that reason. But he couldn't explain why he hadn't taken her yet. Mostly because he didn't know.

"I'm sorry," he mumbled and joined her on the sofa, his eyes shamelessly scanning every inch of her beautiful face. Her high cheekbones and her full lips. Her dark brows and—

"What about this time?" Setting her book down, she met his eyes. There was panic there. Fear. Anger. Every emotion she had every right to feel in his presence.

Evren shrugged, his hands itching to move and push the stray locks from her face.

"I don't know," he finally said with a sigh. "I'm sorry for..." He folded his hands together to keep them from twitching. "I'm sorry for what I am. For what has happened to you."

The words floated between them, and Evren chose not to look at the Enchantress then. He didn't want her to see him as he finally faced his own shameful demons. He'd taken a job that hurt people. People just like her. And he'd taken it knowingly and willingly. Proudly, even. He'd dragged Enchantresses to Valebridge and pocketed the coin selfishly and cowardly. But at the time, it didn't feel so damning. He had the ale to thank for that. For the lack of feeling the last year. But without it, and with *her*, he had nothing to hide behind.

"I grew up in Davenport," Evren continued, still watching the flickering flame of one of the tapered candles lit atop the workbench. "My uncle raised me. He was a fine enough mentor. Kind, albeit a bit strict."

Evren smiled, remembering all the lessons Thaddeous bestowed upon him as a child. How to ration food. How to deal with conflict amongst others. How to fight. How to remain hidden if need be.

"But I was a restless child."

"It seems as though you haven't grown out of that," the Enchantress said.

Evren glanced at her, her blue eyes sparkling in the candlelight. She smiled, and his heart skipped a beat. He knew magick was real all his life. Had witnessed it do wondrous things. Deadly things. But her smile was the kind of magick he never thought existed. The kind that turned the world upside down, then right side up again.

"That's fair," Evren said, now extremely aware of how his leg bounced and his hands twitched even while clasped together. "I always dreamt of something bigger, somewhere other than Teravie. So, when I was eighteen years, I joined the Royal Guard. I put in ten solid years and then King Roman took the throne."

He swallowed down so many memories of the night of the uprising. Or what Roman fed to the army and people as an uprising. He sensed the Enchantress bristle next to him.

"There wasn't—"

"I know." Evren reached out for her hand. He found it through the knit blanket across her lap and she let him grab it. Her brows raised and Evren smiled. He wasn't sure she could be more endearing, but that look, just now, warmed every inch of him.

"I know it wasn't the Enchantresses that started all of this. I know that," he admitted. "But when everything happened in Valebridge, I injured my leg. A Healer, who I'm sure was merely defending herself, snapped it. I've spent a long time blaming her..."

He glanced down, unable to look at the woman next to him, when she squeezed his hand gently. He took it as a sign to keep going. "I spent a long time blaming that Enchantress, *all*

Enchantresses, for my woes the last year, but the reality is, she was defending herself. Against me."

He looked at the Enchantress, waiting for the disgust look he was sure to see.

She frowned but said nothing, her hand still entwined with his.

"I was dismissed from the guard after that and proposed a new position. As captain of the Royal Hunters." He took a deep breath, reclining his head back to look at the stars through the glass roof. With the heavy snow, they were difficult to see, but between the thick flurries, they still shined. "That's when I started to drown myself in ale."

He didn't turn to her, but the sweep of her thumb across the back of his hand told him she was listening.

"Every night. Every morning. Anything to numb the reality that my life would never be the same. I used it as an escape. To end the pain and reality that I was living in. It's cowardly—"

"It's not," the Enchantress said.

He turned to face her. Her eyes were wide and alert.

"We aren't defined by our positions in life," she whispered, her voice beginning to waver. "But by the choices we make within those positions."

She bit her bottom lip, using her free hand to push the hair out of her face and for a moment Evren was disappointed he hadn't done that himself.

"I was born an Enchantress. Given a gift, whether or not I wanted it. But I used that gift to bring joy. Happiness." She looked around her greenhouse.

Evren's eyes never left her face.

"You have a choice too, Evren." She looked at him again. "And I think you're realizing that. How long has it been since you've had a drink?"

The way she said his name made his breath catch in his lungs. In fact, everything about her made his breath catch. Her beauty. Her kindness. But more than anything, her words. Her words had found their way into his heart. His soul. They'd shown him that what he had done wasn't *who* he was. And he could change that. He could change *everything*.

"The day you hurt your shoulder," he said, "I had a drink right before I found you."

He could admit that his mind felt lighter, but it was his body that still felt he'd betrayed it. Still ached and craved and screamed for the cursed liquid.

"I wish I could say I didn't miss it," he admitted.

She nodded slowly.

"It's not much but—"

"It is, Evren." She gripped his hand. "It's extraordinary. You're stronger than you give yourself credit for, Evren."

He smiled, his hand blooming with heat where their skin still connected. There she went again, saying things to him he didn't deserve to hear. He was anything but an extraordinary man, but for her, he'd try. "I've made a lot of poor choices in my life, Enchantress," he whispered, keeping his grip on her hand like steel. "I think it's about time I finally made a good one."

FOURTEEN

TALLULAH DIDN'T MOVE. SHE DIDN'T WANT TO RISK Evren letting her hand go. So she remained still, savoring the heat of his touch and the balm of his words. She waited for her mind to scream at her to run. That he was her enemy. That he hurt people just like her for a living. But the voice in her head never came. And all she could think about was how many outcomes a life had.

One choice and your life would be altered forever. Leaving you grasping at a future you didn't even want just because it was something to hold.

She wanted to be angry with Evren. To curse him for all the hurt he'd done. But what good would it do? Wouldn't showing him kindness and empathy in a life led with cruelty and hate be much more effective? Would he see then just how powerful a choice was?

Evren leaned closer, using his free hand to push the last piece of hair from her face.

Tallulah gasped but didn't move.

"Sorry," he whispered, his face so close they shared the same breaths.

He pulled away, leaving her stomach somersaulting. Disappointment warred with confusion as he slipped his hand out of hers.

They hadn't known each other long. And in that time, they'd tried to kill each other more than once, yet here they were. His words weren't a confession by any means, but they were something. Weren't they?

To tell her he was ready to make a change. A choice.

"Will you be warm enough?" He rubbed his hands together, interrupting her wandering thoughts.

She nodded, still unsure of where her voice had gone. Of what she should say.

He smiled, accepting her nod, and moved away from the sofa.

Glancing at the ceiling, snow piled high onto the glass and by sunrise, she was sure it'd be frozen.

"But maybe it would be better if you stayed closer." She grabbed his arm as her heart threatened to jump out of her chest. "For warmth."

He looked to where her hand met his arm before meeting her gaze.

"If that's what you wish." He slinked back to the sofa.

Her heart raced so quickly she fought the urge to clutch her chest. It slammed and slammed until she thought it might bruise.

She scooted forward toward the edge of the sofa so he could slide in behind her. It was only then, with her back against his chest and his arms cradling her body, that her heartbeat slowed. As if it knew she was finally safe.

"Is this okay?" he whispered against the skin of her neck.

She closed her eyes, wondering how it was possible that they were here when, just a couple of weeks ago she feared for her life in his presence.

But wasn't that how life worked? It changed in an instant. This last year proved just that. So, she didn't question it any further as she sank into him. His arms tightened around her as she said, "Yes. This is okay."

THE SUN STRUGGLED to break through the piles of frozen snow atop the greenhouse roof. The plants furled inward, and the flowers had yet to wake, keeping themselves tucked in tight until another snow storm passed.

Despite Evren's body heat, Tallulah still shivered. Wrapping her arms tighter around herself, she watched as tiny puffs of white expelled from her mouth. Her bones ached and her nose stung.

Evren shifted behind her, his arm tightening around her middle. She held her breath at the movement and glanced downward to where his body connected with hers.

It'd been years since she'd been with a man. Valebridge only allowed interactions between Enchantresses and their designated arrangements with the prospect of bearing a child. She'd met her arranger several times, with never any luck at conceiving.

The thought made her shiver further. A memory she'd suppressed, along with many others. When she couldn't produce a child, they did not grant her another arrangement. She was content with that. She didn't need a partner to fulfill her life, and she certainly didn't need a child to do that. But the way her arranger made her feel used never left her.

Not the way Evren makes you feel.

Squeezing her eyes shut, she pressed down the thought of Evren being anything other than her enemy. A man who swore an oath to the king to capture Enchantresses as if they were wild animals. Before she could think further, she jumped from the sofa, her bare feet stinging against the freezing ground, waking Evren.

"Are you all right?" Sleep lined his voice as he sat up and rubbed at his eyes. His auburn hair was a mess of waves.

"Yes," she mumbled, shame swirling low in her stomach. She couldn't look at him. If the other Enchantresses knew what she was doing while they were locked up... Their magick being stolen... "I'm going out."

"You'll freeze!" Evren jumped from the sofa. "Whatever it is you must do, I'm sure it can wait until the storm passes, it isn't worth the risk."

She turned to face him, to see just how much he worried about his promise of coin walking into the freezing cold.

"Don't worry, Evren, I'm not going to die in the two minutes it'll take me to check the snares." She crossed her arms, mostly for warmth and a touch of impatience. "Your bounty is safe."

His brows knitted together.

"Did you not understand me last night?" He stepped closer, and she felt herself shrink.

She didn't want him to be this close to her. Not again. But it wasn't because she feared him. No, it was the opposite. It was because some part of her *wanted* him to be close. And that was unacceptable.

"I told you I'm done making poor decisions," he whispered.

His thumb met her chin, tilting it slightly to meet his eyes. She waited for her body to recoil. To jump back and hiss at this hunter who had caused so much pain to her people. But she didn't move.

She studied his face. His strong jaw and straight nose. The freckles that danced over his cheeks. The sweat he'd worn across his brow since he saved her had ceased. His hands did not tremble against her skin. Proof that the ale was making its way out of his system, likely with the help of the yarrow root tea she'd insisted he drink.

Her magick stirred, low in her abdomen. Coming back to

life after that damn arrow nearly took her out. But she didn't reach for it. Instead, she pushed it down.

Be still, she whispered to it.

She wasn't ready to use it. Or perhaps it was that she didn't want to.

"And so." She stepped into his touch. Challenging him. She wanted to see how far he'd let her go. How much he could endure of this *witch*.

He didn't step back. Didn't flinch.

"You will *not* be taking me to Valebridge today?" Her stomach flipped as the hand tucked under her chin slid down the soft column of her throat, before landing on the back of her neck.

"Not today," he whispered before sliding his hand from her completely.

Immediately, she missed his touch.

Or was it just companionship she craved?

She didn't push the thought because she simply didn't have time to before Evren placed both of his hands upon her shoulders.

"I'll check the traps," he said, giving her shoulders a squeeze. "You make the tea."

And before she could argue, he slipped past her and out of the door.

FIFTEEN

"How much longer until Davenport?" Markus asked from the back of the caravan. They'd been traveling all morning, and his arse was too sore from the wooden bench he was practically glued to.

"About an hour," the coachman said over his shoulder.

Markus sighed, resting his head against the wall. The back to back snow storms had set them behind almost two weeks, forcing them to stop and camp until it passed. After he stopped at the Jade Guild to check on Evren, he immediately set forth to Davenport.

Turns out, Evren never showed up to see his uncle, Lord Thaddeus. In fact, Thaddeus hadn't heard from him at all. Given their last conversation, this struck Markus as truly bizarre.

First, dismissing two men for merely doing their jobs. Then, to make it all this way and not even check in with Thaddeus? Something didn't sit right and Markus' only hope was that Evren hadn't made it to Valebridge already.

The coachman was right on his word, and an hour later they pulled into a snowy Davenport. Checking in at the Lonely

Seabird Inn, Markus got straight to work calling a meeting with any hunters still in the area.

Back at the Blackwind Tavern, he ordered a round for the six men at his booth before settling in for questioning.

"Tell me again what happened." He gestured to Jasper and Alexander, the two men he'd already interviewed in Copenspire.

They sighed before taking long sips of their ale.

"We already told you," Jasper said. "Captain Fletcher came out of nowhere and demanded we give up our hunt."

"We weren't doing anything wrong, either. He stole her right out from under us," Alexander snarled before downing the rest of his drink.

Jasper nodded, adding nothing to the story.

Markus turned his attention to the other men at the table.

"And you? What have you heard about Captain Fletcher?"

The men looked nervously at their drinks. They were young, not much older than the recruit, Joseph, he spoke with in Copenspire.

"I asked you a question," Markus said with a sigh. "I haven't all night."

The first recruit swallowed, his adam's apple bobbing. "We got word about an hour ago that Captain Fletcher never made it to Valebridge. He's been missing three weeks now, so there should have been plenty of time to make it there."

There was no sense of worry in the recruit's voice, which Markus found odd. Did no one find his disappearance alarming?

"And what of this Enchantress? What was her gift?" Markus pointed his question to Jasper and Alexander again.

They rolled their eyes, clearly tired of the conversation.

"She was a Florecas." Alexander picked with his tongue at something caught in his teeth.

"A Florecas?" Markus asked, a bit bewildered how a wielder of plants managed to best these two men.

"She wasn't just an ordinary Florecas growing magick herbs and shite. She grew vines from her palms," Jasper said, anger creasing his brows. "Was quick, too."

He turned to Alexander for confirmation, who nodded. "We know how it sounds," Alexander said. "But believe me, she's dangerous. It's why we fired the arrow; it was the only way to ensure she couldn't use her magick."

"You could've used the shackles," Markus said, annoyed and ready to be alone in his bed at the inn after several nights of camping in the freezing cold.

"No." Jasper shook head. "There's no way we could have gotten close enough to shackle her."

Markus reclined, resting his head against the back of the wooden booth. "Thank you, you're dismissed."

He ran a hand down his face as the men all left the booth without so much as a goodnight.

After the Lieutenant left and Evren's sudden disappearance, he was somehow the next in charge. He couldn't decide if he enjoyed it or found it incredibly fucking exhausting. He was nowhere near finding Evren, but if the Enchantress was as dangerous as these men claimed, he wouldn't stop until he did.

Sixteen

Evren had lost track of time the last few weeks
with the Enchantress in the greenhouse. At first, it was the
brutal nights of Winter that had forced them to stay close
together, and he hadn't minded one bit. A part of him was
thankful for the freezing cold for that very reason. But Winter
had almost passed, replaced by longer days and warmer nights.
Yet they still sought the other.

"For warmth," the Enchantress had said each night.

"For warmth," he had agreed, knowing well that it was
plenty warm inside the greenhouse now.

Each time the skin of her hand brushed his arm, he thought
he might combust. But he lay perfectly still, letting her settle
against his chest. Letting her decide just how close they'd be.

Every morning, he felt a little lighter. A little stronger
without the ale. Even his leg didn't bother him as much.

He sipped his yarrow root tea; yet another thing he had to
be grateful for. The Enchantress insisted they use the last of her
supply for tea for them to share. And sure enough, it helped
tremendously.

He'd long forgotten his plan to take her to Valebridge as
they settled into a sort of routine.

He knew her magick had come back. She'd flexed her fingers and rubbed her palms together like she was waking the ivy up. She moved differently. More freely. But he could see every so often in her brilliant blue eyes that she was conflicted. But still, she never used it. Never raised her hand against him. He wasn't sure if it was because she knew if she did, more hunters would sense her, or if she truly didn't want to.

He hoped it was the latter. That she was feeling all the same things for him as he did for her. She was all he could think about. Even in his sleep, she consumed his dreams.

Her eyes. Her smile. The sound of her voice.

She hummed a soft tune as she planted more dahlias on the workbench. Evren sat happily on the stone ground, planting a few of his own, sipping his tea. He'd become rather fond of gardening. He smiled, knowing how much shite Markus would give him if he saw him now. But as soon as Markus entered his mind, Evren's stomach soured.

Shite.

Markus would wait for him in Copenspire and when Evren didn't arrive, surely, he'd come looking. How much time had passed? Could it be a month already?

He glanced up at the Enchantress again. Her dark hair hung low down the back of her laced emerald gown. Her eyes were alight with joy as she stuffed another dahlia bulb into a clay pot.

His heart raced thinking of how poorly he'd thought this through. They had been holed up in this greenhouse, and for what? They couldn't stay here long term. They shouldn't even be here *now*. But where would they go? If he were to leave, would she come with him?

Yes. She would join him. Wouldn't she?

He hadn't imagined all the late-night chatter and lingering glances. All the subtle ways she sought to touch his hand or graze his shoulder.

They'd spent the last few weeks after the storm growing a friendship. She loved gardening, nature, and animals.

Evren loved all those things, too.

Perhaps not as vigorously as before he met her, but that was the thing about her. She brought out all the things in him he'd long forgotten. Passion being one of them.

A small bird flew through the cracked door just to the left of the workbench.

"Hello," the Enchantress said with a wide smile. As if she was greeting an old friend.

The bird sang in response.

"Can you speak to them or something?" Evren asked, his eyes wide with bewilderment.

She laughed but didn't turn to him, keeping her focus on the small bird.

"Of course not," she said, and the bird flew off and back out of the door.

She turned to him then, smoothing her skirts. His cheeks warmed under her full attention, but he didn't break her gaze.

"Perhaps if you didn't scowl so often," she said, "they wouldn't mind showing you some affection too."

Their eyes met briefly before she turned. And in them he saw every Enchantress he'd taken to Valebridge. Every life he traded for shillings. Every soul he damned. He couldn't breathe. His chest tightened but then she began to hum again and his shoulders unclenched.

He was hard and she was soft, and he wanted nothing more to be even the slightest bit more like her. To laugh openly. To speak kindly to something so small as a bird without the fear that someone would find him mad.

The last few weeks she'd listened intently when he told stories of his childhood and laughed when he explained how one summer he was determined to fly. Her head tipped back and her eyes closed as she laughed when he explained the wings he made of sticks and leaves.

It was then he'd made a vow to make her laugh as often as he could.

There was no mockery or disgust whenever he mentioned how badly he missed ale. She just held his hand, brushing her thumb over his knuckles. She'd brewed the yarrow root tea and wiped his sweat ridden brow with a cold cloth. The touch intimate enough to make his stomach flip and forget the tremors completely.

He glanced at her again, her back still turned, and his heart raced. He dropped the small shovel he'd been using as his hand began to shake but this time it wasn't because of his need for ale. It was because of his need to keep her safe.

She was worth every challenge. Every risk. And so, a plan formed and he would do just that. Keep her safe.

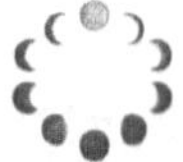

Tallulah hummed as her fingers relished the cold dirt. She added more soil into the pot where the dahlias would grow before she would transplant them to a bigger area of the greenhouse.

Evren worked behind her, planting his own flowers. Something he apparently was keen to back home. She glanced at him over her shoulder. His hair was longer now, and more of a mess than ever. It made her smile as she resumed her work.

She wasn't sure if she believed him or if his sudden interest in gardening was for her sake, but she didn't care. It was endearing to watch him learn her craft. And it was all so simple. So easy. He was here, and she was here and so often she forgot why they met.

The weeks since he'd been here had melted together. She looked forward to waking every day just so they could sip tea together and appreciate the foggy Winter mornings, which now slowly trickled to Spring. She was thankful for each cold night, using it as an excuse to bundle up next to him on the sofa. And even when the weather shifted, she yearned to be closer.

Every moment she was near him, her hand found his. Even if it wasn't her intention. It was as if he was always here. As if they were always—

Tallulah's hands stopped; her dahlia bulbs left forgotten. Her memory came swiftly in, kicking and screaming.

He had *not* always been here. He had a very specific reason. One she was foolish to forget. He had tried to take her to Valebridge. Tried to sell her off. And she had tried to kill him as well. What was it they were truly doing here? Surely, he would have taken her by now. But if he didn't plan to take her to Valebridge, what exactly did he plan to *do*?

"Evren." She kept her back turned to him. Nerves fluttered in her stomach as her dirt-stained hands gripped the edge of the workbench for balance.

"Yes?" His boots scraped against the stone floor.

She cleared her throat and closed her eyes, keeping her back to him. Dreading the question she knew she had to ask. "Are you taking me to Valebridge today?"

Her heart raced as she waited. The laces on her dress suddenly became too tight. The air of the greenhouse, too heavy. Her body warmed as he stepped behind her. She held in a shudder as he bracketed his arms on either side of her, caging her between himself and the workbench.

They'd been close when they slept most nights. But never like this. Never during the day. Especially with her back turned and vulnerable.

And she was afraid.

Not for what he was, a hunter. But for *who* he was. Evren. Her friend. Her...

"Not today, Tallulah," he whispered against her ear. The same words he'd told her again and again. But this time, it was different.

Not today, *Tallulah.*

Tallulah.

In the weeks he'd been here, never once had he called her by her name. Always Enchantress or witch, but never her *name.*

Tallulah.

Her name on his lips spun something inside of her. Not soothing, like she had imagined it would be. It was destruction. It was the end of everything she knew and the beginning of everything she'd never dreamt of.

It set her on fire.

She didn't turn even when his body pressed closer to hers. Her stomach flipped when he brushed his fingers against the bodice of her dress.

"Not tomorrow." He brushed her hair off her neck.

"Nor the next day." She held her breath for fear that if she moved, he would, too.

"Not ever," he whispered before planting a kiss against her neck where her hair had just been.

He kissed her again, this time just beneath her ear, and Tallulah closed her eyes, sucking in a sharp breath. Her lids were heavy when she opened them again. She turned, wanting to study his face.

His green eyes and his messy waves made her heart stop. Time stood still. He was beautiful. Not in the way a rose was beautiful or a sunset, but in the way oceans and mountains were. The kind of beauty you could get lost in. That made you feel like there was so much more to this world than met the eye. Devastatingly.

He'd changed so much in these last few weeks. Not only in the way he looked at her, but in the way he looked at himself. Without the constant stream of ale in his system, he laughed more openly. He spoke with conviction and passion and, above all else; he softened.

She couldn't look at him long enough. She wanted to memorize his face. Count every freckle.

"And why is that?" she dared to ask, no longer fearing his answer. In some way, she already knew it.

"Because," he whispered, his hands moved to her back, pulling her into his chest, "you have shown me kindness in a world rich with cruelty."

Her heartbeat erratically in her chest, but she felt more grounded than ever.

"You asked me before who it was I worshiped. Do you remember?"

She swallowed thickly, unable to think clearly when they were so close. But she did remember. Their first meeting, she'd asked him if not Mother Gaia then who?

"Yes," she managed, locking her eyes with his.

"And I told you no one." Evren pulled back slightly.

Tallulah nodded, words failing her.

"Maybe it was because I hadn't deemed anything worthy of worship."

She frowned, her stomach dropping. She never thought too hard about Evren's lack of faith in Mother Gaia, but in this moment, it hit her. He didn't believe.

Evren's lips dipped to her ear. The heat her body was engulfed with quickly turned to an inferno.

"But I would fall to my knees for you in an instant, Tallulah."

Her breath hitched.

There it was again. Her name on his lips.

But it was so much more than that. It was change and promise and hope.

She rose onto her toes. Lacing her fingers behind his neck, she then pulled him downward. He smelled of fresh rain and pine, and she couldn't help the smile that took over before her lips met his.

The kiss was slow. Cautious. But the way his hands found her back and his body pressed forward showed her just how much he *did* want her. Confidence fueled her next move as she kissed him deeper. Her mouth parted, and with it, his did too.

And then she was lost.

Spiraling to the point of no return. But she didn't care. She wouldn't be the first to break away. Wouldn't let this moment go for fear it would be the last. It couldn't be. Her head spun as her stomach dipped and before she knew it, Evren hoisted her up so she sat on the workbench. His hands, firm against her back.

He reclined, breaking apart their kiss, and so Tallulah held her breath as he scanned her face. Her heart constricted as a flicker of worry crossed his eyes, but then, in an instant, it was gone. And returned was Evren. *Her* Evren and she was lost all over again.

"Tall—"

"Just kiss me, Evren," she whispered, cutting off any voice of reason.

She didn't want to hear it. She just wanted this. Wanted him. He didn't speak again as he closed the gap between them, kissing her deeper than before. She parted her dress to wrap her legs around his waist, and her spine tingled.

His hands ran up her back, then dragged down slowly until they planted firmly at her hips. His lips never left hers, and she decided she'd be perfectly happy if they never did again.

Tallulah opened her mouth, their tongues meeting, sending a thrill through her body. His hands pressed deeper into her, putting the least amount of distance between them.

But it was still too great. Too many obstacles stood in her way. She pulled back, breaking their kiss. Evren watched her, his lids heavy, his breathing ragged.

"What is it?" he asked.

Tallulah smiled at the worry in his voice. She ran her thumb over his bottom lip, something she'd longed to do for ages.

"You're wearing too many clothes," she whispered.

Seventeen

Evren chuckled, but when Tallulah didn't, he knew she was serious.

He took a step backward, already missing the touch of her lips on his. He couldn't believe she'd kissed him. How she could look at him as anything but a monster was beyond him, but he'd given her the space to decide. And she chose to kiss him of all things.

Maybe that made him selfish. But Tallulah had full control here, and they both knew it.

Tallulah.

Saying her name aloud almost felt as good as her lips.

Almost.

Slowly, he unbuttoned his vest, ignoring the glare from his captain's badge as it hit the floor.

Tallulah watched his every move, still positioned atop the workbench. The pink of her lips matched the blush of her cheeks, and it made Evren crazy in the best way knowing he'd been the cause.

His eyes didn't leave hers as he pulled his dark shirt up and over his head before tossing it on the ground. Tallulah's gaze only broke his to trail down his body. She scanned every inch of his exposed chest and abdomen before her eyes finally met his again.

Her gaze froze him in place. His lungs struggled to expand under her scrutiny.

When he didn't move, Tallulah tsked.

"Are you going to remove your pants, or do you need me to do that for you?" she asked with a laugh.

Evren laughed too, breaking him from the spell. His fingers moved with haste, unlacing his pants, and stepping out of them. She smiled and his heart stopped. How could she ask him to do anything when she looked at him like that?

By some miracle, he took a step forward. Then another until he was between her legs again.

"Evren." She leaned forward to meet his mouth.

Their kiss was blazing, and he hated she was still covered. But he knew it would be her choice. She would decide what happens next and he would happily let it stay that way. If him being the one vulnerable made her more comfortable, he'd do it every time.

His hands moved down her body before finding purchase on the tops of her thighs. Her dress had ridden up, exposing her legs, and he relished in the feeling of her skin against his.

She wrapped her legs tighter around his waist, arching her back with each passionate kiss. He broke away, leaving them both breathless.

"Let me do this for you, Tallulah." He pressed his forehead against hers.

She nodded, the corners of her mouth turning up before he dropped to his knees.

As Evren slid between her legs, his hands reached under the skirt of her dress, pulling her undergarments down with him.

He planted soft kisses on the inside of each thigh. Her pulse fluttered; her breaths ragged.

Every touch of his hands, every swipe of his tongue left Tallulah gasping and aching for more. Her head fell backward, her hands planted behind her. If not for them, she was sure she'd fall completely. His mouth was hot against her body as he tasted her and the moans that left her echoed through the small greenhouse.

When she couldn't take it anymore, she tugged his hair, forcing him to stand. He smiled wide, wiping a thumb across his bottom lip, and Tallulah thought she might die at the sight. Before she could think, he picked her up. Her legs wrapped around him as he kissed her deeply. They made their way to the sofa where they'd spent so many of their evenings getting to know each other.

"Should I undo this?" he whispered in her ear as her feet hit the ground. His fingers traced the laces of her gown.

"Yes."

He spun her around, placing a soft kiss on the side of her neck. His fingers worked through the laces, but as her dress fell to the ground, the world seemed to slow. Tallulah's instinct was to cover herself. It was still midday and every part of her was exposed. But as Evren's hands traced the outlines of her curves, as his mouth kissed the side of her neck, she didn't care how exposed she was. She wanted him to see all of her, the way she'd seen all of him. It'd been a very long time since she'd felt powerful. Worthy. But in this moment, she felt nothing but.

Turning, she glanced up at him. His green eyes met hers with a softness that weakened her knees more than his kiss. She stood on her toes and laced her fingers around the back of his neck again, forcing him to meet her mouth.

Just before he kissed her, he pressed his forehead against hers. He didn't say a word, but there wasn't any to say. This was madness. Foolish and dangerous. But they didn't care. Because in all of life's uncertainty, this was one thing they knew to be true. Whatever reason they'd fallen for each other was reason enough to risk everything.

One look and that was it. The final threshold that held them together. That single look was both of their undoing.

Tallulah couldn't kiss Evren fast enough. She wanted more. She wanted everything. They toppled onto the sofa, Evren on top of her. His hands were in her hair, on her body. Over her breasts and between her legs. Circling between her thighs, forcing small moans with each swipe of his thumb. His body was hard on top of hers, but she arched her back, encouraging him. His hand slid away for a moment as he put himself in place.

"Are you sure?" he whispered. Giving her a chance to change her mind. But rationality had long since passed.

"Yes."

She pushed her hips forward again. His free hand fisted her hair as he slid slowly inside of her. Tallulah's eyes rolled closed at the same time Evren let out a deep moan.

"*Tallulah.*" Again, he pulled back, and even slower than before, he inched forward.

"Say it again," she rasped.

He smiled, his eyes crinkling in the corners.

"Tallulah." He pushed forward slowly.

"Tallulah." He kissed her deeply before moving to her neck and kissing her there.

She gasped, needing more friction. More of him. Their eyes locked and that alone was enough to force a moan from her lips.

Her hips moved in time with his, her hands placed firmly on his back, her legs wrapped tightly around his waist. His fingers kneaded and pulled through her hair, his other hand grasping her chin as he kissed her fiercely.

She couldn't recall a moment ever feeling like this. As if she didn't get *more* of him, she would cease to live. Evren sensed her growing need, quickening his pace, deepening his movements.

"Don't stop," Tallulah said, her breaths too quick. Her body, too hot.

He kissed her harder as he moved his hips. Her need coiled inside of her. His hands found hers, pulling them above her head, interlocking their fingers, holding them tightly but tenderly all at the same time. His teeth grazed her neck and as they did, she lost all control.

Her pleasure shot through her, in every cell of her body. He pulled back, his eyes scanning her face. She may have shouted his name, but she couldn't be sure. The room spun as she came back to and moments later, Evren joined her, burying his face in the crook of her neck as he found his own release.

They stayed there for a few moments. Lost in bliss. Tallulah quite enjoyed the weight of Evren on top of her, her legs still wrapped around his hips. Lifting his face, he met her eyes before he leaned forward and kissed her softly. Slowly. His teeth pulled at her bottom lip. He didn't say a word as he rose from the sofa and walked away. Naturally, doubt formed in the back of her mind. Perhaps this was a mistake.

She sat up, covering her chest with her arms. But when she stood to find her dress, Evren appeared before her. Pants on, slightly unlaced, but no shirt.

"Let me help you." He dropped to his knees, forcing Tallulah to recline back on the sofa.

It was the second time today this hunter knelt before her, and she couldn't deny the power it made her feel. She studied his broad shoulders and the freckles across them that matched those on his face.

He brought a towel from the workbench, slowly cleaning her up. Each swipe of the towel and brush of his hands made Tallulah's stomach flip. When he was done, he slid his shirt over her head. It smelled of him. Of rain and pine and earth. She wrapped it tighter around herself, still dazed by the events of the afternoon. Wishing she could stay wrapped up in his shirt and his arms.

"Thank you," she whispered, completely unsure what to do now.

Evren smiled. His eyes held a hint of mischief, and his hair was tousled from Tallulah's fingers. He slid onto the sofa beside her, pulling her onto his lap with her back to his chest. Her stomach dipped as she rested her head against him. His fingers softly twisted her hair into a braid, occasionally stopping to grasp her chin and turn it toward him for a slow kiss.

They spoke little the rest of the day. But it wasn't the silence that left Tallulah worried. It was how comfortable the silence was. Comfortable and content. As if it were always meant to be this way. She and Evren in the greenhouse. With the cold nights and the foggy mornings. With the stories and pine needle tea and his arms wrapped around hers. Him washing and braiding her hair.

But it wasn't always meant to be this way. It was *never* meant to be this way. And she was a fool to think there would ever be a future like this. The memory of the pleasure they'd just had washed away and replaced with what she *should* have been feeling all along.

Fear.

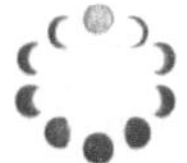

THE NEXT MORNING Evren found himself with Tallulah tucked in tightly to his chest, her hair still braided from yesterday, and the greenhouse dimly lit from the early morning sun. Today was like any other day that he'd woken up to, except it wasn't.

They'd been together, and it had changed everything.

Even before that, Evren knew what his heart wanted. It was his brain that took longer to catch up. Logic and reason had always been his leading emotions, but with her, neither of those seemed to matter.

Especially now that she'd been vulnerable with him. Had let him see all of her, had *wanted* him to see.

There was no going back. He had fallen deeply. Slowly, but deeply. He couldn't pinpoint the exact moment, but he imagined it began the day she let him go. Let him live even when she knew what his intentions were.

She often spoke about being a Florecas. How it was not a magick deemed useful to anyone but the flowers she grew. And so many times in the last few weeks he'd wanted to tell her that her magick was so much more than plants and flowers. It was softness in the face of brutality. It was brightness on a gloomy day and joy in the wake of chaos. It was her passion for all living things and her empathy for those that maybe didn't deserve it. Like him. *Especially* him.

His stomach flipped as Tallulah moaned in her sleep. A sound he wouldn't mind hearing every day of his life. He leaned down and placed a kiss on her temple, soft enough that she wouldn't wake, but firm enough to wash away the worry forming between her brows. Not that he didn't want her to wake, but that she deserved the rest.

The rest of the afternoon yesterday had been quiet. Quiet but not uncomfortable. But he missed her laugh. Missed her voice, even if it had only been a few hours. He remained still behind her. Letting her sleep and letting himself form the plan he'd started yesterday. The plan to keep them safe.

His mind drifted briefly to Davenport. To the pub and the ale that, only weeks ago, dictated his life. His every waking moment. But with the ale cleared from his system, he could never imagine going back to that. She had helped him even when she hadn't realized she was doing so. But maybe she had realized, and she never said. Never made him feel poorly for the choices that led him to the withdrawals.

He breathed in the scent of her, floral and sweet, his arms wrapping tighter around her waist. He was determined to be a better man because of Tallulah Hollow. *For* her.

He would never let anything bad happen to her again.

Shivers caused Tallulah to wake. She'd gotten used to the firm warmth of Evren's body behind her and when he was no longer there, she sat up with a start.

She glanced around the greenhouse. It was empty aside from her plants slowly coming to life in the morning sun. Evren's shirt still hung loosely around her, so she pulled it tighter. Taking a deep inhale of the pine and earth scent.

"Oh, you're awake." Evren's voice sounded from behind her.

She turned to see him balancing her teakettle, two mugs, and scrambled quail eggs on a wooden tray. Still shirtless. She smiled, knowing how poor of a cook he was from a previous failed attempt, but the look of determination on his face made her heart warm.

"I made us some..." he glanced down at the scrambled mess.

He must be cold. But if he was, he didn't show it, and she certainly didn't mind the view.

"It smells lovely," Tallulah lied, not wanting to hurt his feelings.

He came to sit beside her, handing her a mug of tea. She drank slowly, watching him over the edge of her mug. His hands no longer twitched as they had before. Instead, they were a new kind of nervous. It was endearing watching him try to impress her. Like he had any reason to. She was already his in a way.

"I'll take that." Tallulah reached for the tray and set it on the ground. Evren's smile left a sensation low in her stomach, so she turned her head and focused on her tea.

She didn't regret for one moment what they'd done yesterday. Doing it again was all she could think about in the most maddening way. But she knew better than to imagine they could have any sort of life together.

Even if Evren made promises to her, that didn't suddenly mean the world would change. Outside of the greenhouse, through the woods that separated her from Davenport, was the ugly truth. King Roman still sought Enchantresses and there were plenty of other men willing and ready to take her in. The tea in her stomach sat like lead.

"Tell me what you're thinking." Evren placed his empty mug onto the stone floor. "Or would you rather me tell you what I'm thinking?"

She turned to face him, that damn smile she had witnessed so rarely over the last few weeks and those green eyes sweeping her away again.

"You first." She bent down to place her mug on the floor as Evren just had.

He bit his bottom lip, as if contemplating where to start. What to say. She couldn't blame his lack of words. She had nothing clear or concise to say either. Only that what she felt for him was...

"I don't regret yesterday," he finally said; he spoke so softly, like what he had to say hurt. She glanced at him again. "But I understand if you...have some reservations. But I meant what I said. About it being time to make some right decisions. Choices."

"Evren—"

"Listen," he said, his brows furrowing. "I'm tired of living my life for other people. Tired of hurting people. The moment I met you, I knew my life would change. Maybe it took me longer than I'd hoped to see which way it would change, but every part of me sees you and more than anything wants you to see me back. I choose you, Tallulah. I choose this."

If it wasn't for the massive panic rising in her, Tallulah may have noticed the other emotions begging to come forth. Joy and hope. But it was all drowned by the voice in her head. The voice of reason.

"Choosing me means going to war, Evren. We're not equipped for that. I will be hunted the moment we leave this greenhouse and if the royal guard knew you aided me…" She bit her lip, guilt trickling in as it always did. "I would never ask you—"

"You aren't asking me," he said a bit more firmly. His hand found hers, their fingers interlocking. "I'm choosing this. *You*. And I would do it over again. I'd go to war in every lifetime if it meant coming home to you at the end."

His thumb swiped the back of her hand, sending a shiver across her body. Her hand squeezed his for the sake of making sure he was real. That *this* was real. But she couldn't let him choose her, could she? It would be a risk to his life, and she wasn't sure if she was willing to do that. But the way he looked at her now. With admiration. With longing. She couldn't imagine any other outcome than the one where they left together.

"It's not a good idea," she finally said, ignoring the desperate feeling to climb on top of him here and now. To claim him again.

"What is it you're so afraid of?" he asked, genuine worry transforming his features.

Tallulah scoffed, pulling her hand away.

"Have you had such a privileged life that you don't know fear?" Her voice had risen, and she wasn't sure if it was anger or frustration laced in her tone. The better question was what *wasn't* she afraid of?

"Yes," Evren said without a moment's hesitation, rubbing his palms together. "I have lived a privileged life." He glanced at her. Her brows relaxed as he spoke, his deep voice settling something inside of her.

"I've never had to fear walking down the street or into a tavern. Have never once had to question my safety simply because of who I am." Her eyes welled with tears, but she didn't look away. "I have lived a privileged life, Tallulah. I've been naïve to see the world so small. To only see what was right in front of me. To only believe what I was told and never question otherwise."

He took her hand again, and she let him. The warmth of his touch was enough to let the tears she'd held back fall. Dropping quietly down her cheeks, she ignored the salty taste as they hit her lips.

"But now," he continued, his fingers tightening around her hand. "Now, I see *you*. How beautiful you are. How kind and compassionate. I see the hate that's been burning through Teravie. Wildfires of lies leaving a permanent scar upon our country and for what? Power?"

He shook his head, his cheeks reddening to match his hair.

"So, yes." He looked at her again, his face softening as he did. "I have lived a privileged life, and I will continue to because our country is corrupt."

He slid closer to her so that their legs touched. Her breath hitched.

"But I promise you," he whispered. "I will do everything within my privilege to help you. To help others. It is the least I can do and I'm ashamed I haven't seen the truth sooner. But I see it now. I see you."

She let go of his hand and instead climbed onto his lap. Her legs straddled either side of him, her fingers lacing around the back of his neck.

"So, you choose me." She tilted her head forward so her lips barely brushed his.

"Yes," he said with the utmost surety.

"But we can't stay here."

Just this morning, she intended to tell him they should part ways, but she couldn't bring herself to say it. Not after everything he'd said. Not after everything she'd felt yesterday. Felt now.

Evren brought his bottom lip through his teeth, his eyes fixing on her mouth for a moment. Running her fingers through his hair, heat blossomed in her abdomen.

"I think I know where we can go." Evren dragged his hand down her spine. She shivered at his touch, leaning closer to him. "Somewhere we'll both be safe."

Her brows knitted together. There wasn't anywhere in Teravie she'd truly be safe. But those were questions for another time. Now, all she could think about was her body on top of his. The hands that were dancing along her back. The lips she so eagerly wanted to claim.

"We can't just hide while others suffer," she challenged, her hips rolling forward. Evren's eyes fluttered closed for a moment at the movement.

"I know," he said with a nod. "But we must start somewhere. And if we're to help others, we must help ourselves first."

Tallulah nodded, pushing her hips selfishly forward again. Her eyes fixed on his mouth.

"I'll leave tomorrow."

This doused the heat between herself and Evren in an instant.

"Leave?" She pulled herself backward.

"Yes." His hands ran up and under the shirt—*his* shirt still on her. Her skin pebbled under this soft touch. "I'll head to Davenport and send word to my uncle. It's the only place we can go—"

"How do I know..." She looked away, her words lost. She wanted to trust Evren. And she supposed she'd trusted him all these weeks. Her magick was back, but she hadn't once thought to use it. She'd never once felt she *needed* to use it. Not like when they first met.

"I'll keep you safe." His arms wrapped tightly around her. "I promise."

His eyes locked on hers and she found no hint of deceit. No

lies. That voice deep within her mind screamed at her, but she ignored it and leaned forward. She placed her lips on his and it was the final push into the descent into madness.

The kiss wasn't soft like yesterday's had been. She didn't want soft. She wanted to devour him. She wanted to kiss him so deeply they could both forget what they faced outside the greenhouse.

Evren moaned against her mouth, his hands sliding further over her before he pulled the shirt from her completely.

The crisp morning air bit against her skin, but she hardly felt it. All she could feel was him. His confessions. His promises. She was drunk on them.

She slid off him momentarily so he could discard his pants. As soon as he did, she was back on his lap. The friction of their bodies together set every nerve of hers on fire. She would never tire of the way his breath changed each time she touched him. Or the sound he made when she slowly slid herself onto him. She wanted to savor this, but the nagging voice in her mind reminded her that time was the one thing they didn't have.

Evren kissed along her neck, and she moaned, her head falling back. Rocking her hips forward, she braced her hands on the back of the sofa as he clung to her hips. His fingers dug into her flesh while his lips trailed kisses over her body. Their releases erupted between them, and despite the chill in the air, their bodies were slick with sweat. Reluctantly, she pulled herself from him as they both took up their normal places on the sofa. Evren at the back and Tallulah tucked carefully to his front.

Evren, breaths still heavy, brought his arms around her, caging her in.

"You're beautiful, Tallulah."

Darkness still covered the greenhouse as Evren woke and dressed himself. He bent down, brushing a kiss to Tallulah's brow. She sighed in her sleep before turning away from him. He had no doubts that he was doing the right thing by leaving to send word to his uncle. But still, in his heart, he worried about what might happen while he was away. Who might find her.

He didn't have a choice, though. She couldn't come to Davenport with him. It was too much of a risk. Outside of Valebridge, Davenport housed the largest station of royal guards in all of Teravie.

She couldn't be seen.

And they wouldn't make it all the way to the Jade Guild without a horse and supplies. So, leaving this early to beat the morning rush in the city was the best decision. He'd send a page to his uncle and hope he'd receive the message in time.

He looked to Tallulah again, pulling the blanket over her before heading for the door.

EIGHTEEN

Tallulah knew Evren left that morning for Davenport, but it didn't make his absence any easier. She awoke with a hole in her chest. A longing in her heart. It'd been a month now of each other's company and every moment without him felt too quiet.

She quickly dressed and braided her hair before finding a bag to pack a few of her things. As she reached for her favorite notebook, a piece of parchment folded in half fluttered to the ground.

Tallulah smiled, knowing Evren must've left her a note. She sank to the ground, pressing her back against the wall of the greenhouse before she opened it.

Tallulah, the captor of my heart,
Meet me as the moon falls and the sun
begins to rise. In the place where the forest
meets the sea. If you begin to doubt where your
feet are going, just listen to the call of my heart,

for it calls only for you. I'll wait for you there.
I'll wait for you always.
    All the stars,
    Evren

She read the note three more times before clutching it tightly to her chest.

The captor of my heart.

Her smile widened as she leapt to her feet. It was only an hour from sunrise and so she would need to hurry.

Of course, she knew exactly where Evren wanted to meet. It was the same place where he'd rescued her from those two hunters. The cliffs where the forest meets the sea, just as he'd said. The place where everything changed between them.

Tallulah scrambled for the last of her belongings before pulling on her boots and Evren's cloak that he'd left for her. With a last glance around the room, she blew her plants a kiss goodbye.

A tiny dose of magick dispersed through the air from her fingertips. Gold and iridescent, the light floated through the greenhouse as it touched the tip of each plant, enchanting them to stay forever green.

She knew it wasn't wise to use her magick, but she wasn't afraid. Not anymore. She was leaving for good.

Her smile faded, knowing how much she'd miss it here. But the hope for the future was too bright to reconsider. With a final whispered goodbye, she turned and headed out into the darkness.

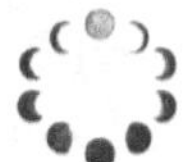

THE BLACKWIND TAVERN mocked Evren with each step into the city.

Even in the dim light of the streetlamps, the building loomed over him. He kept his eyes to the ground, but the tavern watched him with a scrutiny he didn't like as he made his way to the Lonely Seabird Inn.

He wouldn't look at the tavern, yet.

Wouldn't give it the satisfaction even if he knew he'd have to go there before morning for his coin. He'd gotten to know the barkeep well and doing so had earned him a strong box in the back for his earnings. But at this time of night, the urge was more powerful than ever. Even still, he kept his head low.

First the inn, then the tavern, then Tallulah.

It took every bit of his strength to pass by the Blackwind, but when he reached the Lonely Seabird's front door, he let out a sigh of relief.

One step closer.

He didn't know the innkeeper well, but had heard rumors from being stationed there in the past that he was a man of many talents. One of which was discretion. Which was exactly what Evren and Tallulah would need if they were to make it to the Jade Guild safely.

The wooden door creaked as Evren opened it and stepped inside. The immediate warmth from the fireplace stung his frozen cheeks, but he was grateful for it. His heart lurched for a moment, thinking of how Tallulah would soon be out in this cold. But it was for the best that she didn't come to Davenport.

"What can I do you for?"

Evren shook his head at the voice, clearing it of the worry he had for Tallulah.

The innkeeper sat behind a large oak counter. His thinning gray hair swept to the side as if to give the illusion of thickness. Tiny, gold-rimmed spectacles sat barely on his nose. His thick, gray brows pushed together as Evren stood silently in the foyer.

"Are you hard of hearing?" the man asked again.

"No." Evren took a step toward the counter. "Sorry, been a long night."

Though a quick glance out the inn windows reminded him night faded and morning would soon take its place. He needed to hurry. He cast the innkeeper a quick smile, which was left unreturned.

"You may remember me—"

"Get a lot of patrons, don't flatter yourself," the man said in a gruff tone. Reclining in his chair, he crossed his arms and watched Evren over those ridiculously small glasses.

"Right." Evren rubbed his hands together. "Anyway, I'm Captain Fletcher. I was here about a month ago swearing in the recruits for the—"

"Oh yes." The man leaned forward, bracing his elbows on the counter. "I do remember you. Thaddeus' boy."

The innkeeper's eyes narrowed, scouring Evren's face. Evren hid the flinch at being called his uncle's. Instead, he focused on his task.

First the inn, then the tavern, then Tallulah.

"How long will you be here this time, hunter?"

"I'm not staying." Evren leaned closer so he could lower his voice. "I've been told you can acquire..." he glanced around the foyer. Still empty. "You can help me acquire a few things for travel. A horse, a weapon, some supplies. Discretion about me being here."

Evren tapped his fingers restlessly against the oak counter-top. The innkeeper said nothing as he pulled a pipe from the breast pocket of his gray wool sweater and stuck it between his teeth.

"Am I in the right place?" Evren's annoyance showed in his voice now and finally, the man before him smiled around the pipe.

"Sure, hunter," he said. "I'll have your things ready by tomorrow—"

"I need it by dawn," Evren said in a forced whisper. "Time is...of the essence."

"It will cost you." The man's smile widened as if he took immense joy in the proposition.

"It's no matter, I have the coin. I'll fetch it for you as soon as you can promise arrangements will be made by sunrise."

The man watched Evren again before pulling his pipe from his teeth.

"You have my word." He dipped his chin.

Evren nodded, taking a step backward.

"Thank you," Evren whispered before finally turning away. All he needed was the coin to pay the innkeeper, and then he'd be ready to meet Tallulah. His shoulders relaxed, knowing he was one step closer to getting her to safety. One step closer to his life—

"Evren?" He froze in place at the voice. He didn't need to turn to know who it was, and his heart dropped dramatically as the man spoke again. "Evren?"

Turning, he couldn't hide the shake of his hands as the man stepped closer.

"Hello, Markus."

Nineteen

"Where have you been?" Markus closed the gap between them and encased Evren in a tight hug.

Evren grimaced. Markus smelled of ale and sweat. No surprise given how late it was, or rather how early, but it made Evren's face pucker. As Markus pulled away, Evren took a step back.

"You know how chatty my uncle gets. Conversation didn't go as planned, however," Evren said, the lie thick in his throat. "Figured I'd come back here and start fresh on a hunt before meeting you in Copenspire."

He smiled, running a hand nervously through his hair. He hated lying to Markus. Hated the look on his face, which told him he *knew* he lied. But he didn't have a choice. He trusted Markus with most things. But this...this was different. Tallulah's life was on the line and he couldn't gamble whether Markus would help the situation or hurt it.

"Your uncle, you say?" Markus swayed lightly on his feet. "Interesting."

He laughed, stumbling forward to grasp Evren on the shoulder. The stench of ale was potent as he leaned in toward

Evren's ear. Evren's stomach lurched at the scent. The need twitching and whispering throughout his body.

"Rumor around here is you stole yourself a little lass." Markus pulled back, removing his hand from Evren's shoulder. Evren stood, unmoving, as Markus searched his face for the truth.

"I don't know what you mean," Evren said with a smile. "Now come on, let's get a drink."

It's the last thing he wanted to do, but he was desperate to get away from Markus' questions and knowing eyes. He turned to head out the door, but before he could make it more than a few steps, Markus' hand landed on his shoulder again and pulled him around.

"What are you hiding, Evren." Markus glanced toward the front desk.

Evren followed his eyes to find the counter empty, the innkeeper gone to fulfill the task Evren had assigned him. He met Markus' eyes again and guilt lined his insides.

"We need to talk somewhere more private," Evren whispered. Doubt sank its teeth deep in his bones. Could he trust Markus? Or would he see what Evren had done and turn him in? Or worse, would he hurt Tallulah?

Markus straightened, suddenly more sober than he was mere moments ago.

"Let's go." Markus turned and walked up the creaky wooden stairs and reluctantly, Evren followed.

"FUCK," Markus said for the third time. "Tell me again how this happened?"

Evren sighed, his knee bouncing rapidly as he sat in an upholstered chair in Markus' room. They'd been discussing this for nearly thirty minutes and time was running out. It would be dawn soon and he had so much to do. He needed to get his coin. Needed to get the supplies. The horse.

"Evren," Markus snapped, pulling him from his stupor. "Tell me again."

"I've already told you everything." Evren stood from the chair and headed for the window. The dark blue curtains were musky as he pulled them aside to glance at the sky. Purple and gray swam together as dawn quickly made its approach.

"I don't have time to repeat myself." Evren yanked the curtains shut. "Either you're with me, or you aren't."

"What the fuck does that even mean?" Markus shouted.

"Keep your voice down," Evren hissed. "You don't need to do anything other than what I already explained. Tell Lieutenant Benedict that my uncle has fallen ill. Tell him I had to leave the hunt to take on my responsibilities at home."

It wasn't the greatest lie, but it's all Evren could come up with in the time he had. With his uncle's position as Lord of the Jade Guild, he doubted the Lieutenant would question it.

Evren joined Markus on the bed, the two of them sitting side by side. Markus held his head in his hands, as if what he heard was blasphemy.

"Markus, look at me." Slowly, Markus pulled his fingers through his blonde hair and faced Evren. "I know what I'm asking is a lot, but if you knew her—"

"She's an Enchantress, Evren," Markus groaned. "Do you really think she has feelings for you? Think about it, brother."

He tapped Evren's temple a bit too hard.

"She's using you. She's probably halfway across the Trinity Forest by now. You *let* her get away."

"No." Evren shook his head as he contained a laugh. "You don't know Tallulah. She would never use me—"

"You've gone mad," Markus said with a laugh. "How do you know her magick isn't making you feel this way? How can you trust her!"

"Because I just *do*. I can't explain it and I know how it

sounds. But as my friend, my *oldest* friend, please do this for me." He reached for Markus' shoulder and gave it a squeeze. "Please."

Markus rolled his eyes, his head falling back to face the ceiling. After expelling a long breath, he looked at Evren again.

"Fine," he said. "I'll make sure the Lieutenant knows you've gone. And if anyone asks about the Enchantress Jasper and Alexander found, I'll tell them she...got away somehow. Fuck, I don't know." He sighed, throwing his hands in the air. "I don't know, but I'll figure it out."

"Thank you." Evren pulled him in for a quick hug and patted him on the back. "I must go, meet me at the Jade Guild. There's much we need to discuss. The hunt being one of them."

Markus frowned but Evren turned and rushed to the door of the room. Dawn would be here in an hour. And in an hour, he'd be with Tallulah again and their life could begin.

"Evren," Markus said, his voice wavering.

Evren turned to face him, his hand already on the handle of the door, ready to sprint out of the room and toward her.

"Are you sure about this?"

Without hesitation, Evren nodded before he said, "I'm sure."

DESPITE THE UNPLEASANT demeanor of the innkeeper, he stayed true to his word. As soon as Evren left Markus, he went straight to the Blackwind Tavern to tap out his coin. The trade was made in an alley between the inn and the cobbler next store.

The innkeeper said nothing as he swapped the reins of the horse for the bag of Evren's coin. His hand flexed when he passed the bag over. He'd almost saved enough to take a ship to

Scandavi or even farther. But there was no way he had enough for Tallulah as well, and there was *no way* he was leaving without her.

"Thank you." Evren pulled the horse closer to him. He checked the saddlebags briefly, ensuring the supplies they'd need to venture into the woods for several days were there. Satisfied, he extended his hand. The innkeeper watched him, not offering any words, before gripping his hand in a firm shake.

Evren mounted the horse, and the faintest slice of sunlight cut through the dark sky. He was running behind.

"Good luck, Captain Fletcher," the innkeeper said, startling Evren.

He glanced back at him, just as he raised a pipe to his teeth. Nodding, he turned for the square, heeling the horse in the sides to make it to Tallulah as quickly as possible.

Money well spent. The horse raced through Davenport and through the forest until the cliff side where he'd saved Tallulah came into view.

Almost there.

Evren sighed, unclenching his fists from the reins for the first time since he'd left the city.

He was sure she'd know where to meet him. The sea and the earth collided perfectly here, their meeting seamless and endless all at the same time. He only wished he wasn't late. The cold was bitter, causing an ache in his wounded leg. He thought of Tallulah traveling by foot and was relieved again that he'd left her his cloak.

The mare's dark coat glistened under the sun as Evren tied her reins to a nearby tree. His breaths were visible, tiny clouds of white. He cupped his hands and breathed into them a few times for extra warmth as he scanned the area for any sign of Tallulah.

But the water was unusually still. The leaves, unruffled. The muddy paths, mostly unturned.

He took several laps around the trees, taking the time to

peer over the cliff side. Relief and worry warred when he didn't see her on the other side, where the jagged rock lay below.

She is just running behind. Just as he was that morning.

After checking the small fishing shanty, he found a dry spot against a large oak tree and sat, watching the distant waves ripple across the dark gray water.

An hour passed and Evren's worry became a panic.

"Tallulah!" he called into the woods. He didn't give a damn if anyone heard him.

"Fuck," he mumbled when he got no response.

Quickly, he untied the horse and climbed into the saddle, intent on venturing all the way to the greenhouse.

A scream sounded in the distance. His heart stilled.

Then another, and another.

He knew that scream because he'd heard it more than once.

"Go!" He pressed his heels into the mare until they were bolting straight toward the noise. Straight toward Tallulah.

"PLEASE." Tallulah struggled to breathe through the bruised ribs she was sure she had. She clutched her sides, burying her face into the dirt before the men could kick her again.

"On your feet, witch."

She pressed her body further and further into the earth, begging Mother Gaia, begging anyone to listen to her pleas.

Tallulah should've known they'd find her. The hunters who Evren had saved her from. But as soon as she passed the threshold of the forest, there they were. As if they were waiting. As if they *knew* she'd be there. Her mind quickly sprang to Evren. He was the only other person who knew their plan.

He wouldn't do this, would he?

"I said on your feet." One of the hunters slammed his boot against her ribs again.

She screamed, the crack of bone echoed through the distant trees. Before she could catch her breath, she was hauled to her feet. One man on either side, their firm grip on her elbows a momentary distraction from the pain she felt in her ribs. Her knees gave way, her legs dragging limply behind her as they pulled her toward Davenport. Her heart raced and her head spun.

This is it.

Twenty

Tallulah had been in this position before, she remembered through her waning consciousness. Her head bobbed and rolled as the men pulled her through the dirt and mud. Through the haze and the blinding pain, Tallulah thought for a moment she heard a voice.

His voice.

But as quickly as it came, it was gone.

Just a memory.

Her eyelids scratched and begged to close. Her vision blurred and quickly she relented. There wasn't any use to keeping herself awake for whatever happened next. But there it was again.

"I told you to unhand her."

Tallulah called on every bit of strength she could find to lift her head. She wouldn't believe it until she saw it.

Saw him.

Her vision doubled and her head swam, but as her eyes focused, she let out a muffled cry.

Evren stepped closer. A short sword drawn. She'd never seen him with such a weapon.

"Do you need me to repeat it a third time, gentlemen," Evren said, his voice deep and low. "Unhand her."

His lip snarled, and briefly, his eyes dashed to hers. Rage contorted his features as he noted the blood spilling from her nose. The bruises under her dress would be a discovery for later.

"Evren." The hunter on her right tightened his grip around her arm. "You know very well what you've done. You have no authority here anymore."

They didn't address him as captain this time and her heart lurched for all he'd sacrificed for her. All he was willing to do.

"Lieutenant will know, everyone will know." The man speaking dropped Tallulah's arm, leaving her with just one captor. Evren readied himself into a fighting position as the hunter drew closer.

"You're an embarrassment to the hunt," he spat, completely disregarding Evren's weapon. As if he didn't think he'd use it. "You're an embarrassment to yourself."

Tallulah's head was heavy, but she wouldn't let it fall. She kept her eyes locked on Evren. Watched his every move. His every breath. She waited for him to realize what he'd done. To realize that she wasn't worth the risk, the sacrifice.

But his face never faltered.

He took a deep breath and peered around the guard again.

And there it was.

All the confirmation she needed lied within his eyes. He didn't regret his decision. He chose her. And he'd do it again. The look was everything she needed and when he dipped his chin in the slightest; she knew what he asked. She knew what he wanted.

Tallulah closed her eyes, taking a deep but labored breath. She pushed past the pain. Past the fear that had kept her caged in that greenhouse for the last year. She opened her eyes and looked into Evren's and saw her future. She saw herself. How powerful she could be. How important she was.

The hunter still beside her had dropped his hand, clearly

more invested in Evren. So, with his distraction and the man she loved across from her believing in her, she raised her hands.

Bloodied and caked in mud. She raised them higher and higher until she heard the hunter next to her gasp. But before he could make right on his mistake of letting her go, she flicked her wrists upward.

Tallulah had known the moment she gained her magick from Mother Gaia she'd be a disappointment.

A disappointment to her mother.

A disappointment to herself.

Tallulah never felt useful. Never clever or quick to learn things. She'd kept to herself and her books and her garden. She'd lived a life so many would consider simple. But in all the simple moments she'd lived, she'd forgotten how *powerful* simple could be.

Planting a seed was simple. But to nurture it, care for it, watch it grow and evolve was powerful. To read was simple. A skill so many had. Yet, there's power in words. In imagination and declarations. There's power in picking up a story and not just reading it. But *living* it. In your mind and in your heart. Your soul.

Her magick was simple. She could conjure any plant she pleased. But here she was. Calling upon a simple ivy and watching it wrap around the throat of her two assaulters. So distracted by Evren and his blade, the hunters paid no mind to the girl who could simply grow plants.

Underestimating her would be their last, fatal mistake.

Her energy faded quickly with her injuries, but she didn't stop until the ivy had tightened all the way around their throats. Until they dropped to their knees. Until they stopped strug-gling completely and lay limply beneath her hands. It was only then she dropped her hands to her sides before abruptly falling to her knees.

Evren was there in an instant, as he always was.

"Tallulah," he breathed against her skin as he scooped her up into his arms. His grip was firm around her as he carried her away and she winced at the pressure on her ribs.

"Evren!" a man shouted from behind them.

Evren froze.

His arms tightened even more as he turned. It was difficult to make out his face, but the man stepped closer and his blonde hair glowed in the sun.

"You sent them," Evren whispered, not letting Tallulah go.

The man nodded, running a hand down his face.

"I didn't think they'd do this," the man said, his voice shaking. He looked to Tallulah but quickly looked away.

"You betrayed me, Markus," Evren spat, his body beginning to tremble.

"I only sent them to look for *you*! I didn't think—"

Tallulah's body softly landed upon the dew-soaked grass. She sucked in a breath at the sharp pain to her sides, but she didn't dare take her eyes off Evren.

She would never again.

"Their blood is on your hands." Evren stepped closer to the man called Markus. "*You* did this, not her."

The man shook his head, peering over his shoulder at the two men lying on the ground. "I was trying to save you, Evren. Trying to keep you here. Trying to rid your mind of the poison she's been feeding you."

Evren took a step backward, angling his body in front of her.

"Go." Evren scooped her back in his arms. They were warm, a comfort. She could weep from the scent of him alone.

Her eyes were heavy again, the world around her spinning.

"Leave now before one more body lies lifeless on the ground."

Tallulah shivered at his words. At what she'd done.

She cracked her eyes open one last time before they turned. Markus, she thought that was his name, gave her a wry look before returning his focus to Evren.

"I'll go," Markus whispered. "I'm sorry, Ev. I just—"

Evren's body flinched beneath her, but he turned before he could hear another word, leaving the town and Markus in the past.

Evren secured her to the horse, ensuring her comfort before settling in behind her. He wrapped his arms around her middle to grab the reins and kissed her once on the cheek. "You'll be okay now, Lu," he whispered.

Her head fell backward, meeting his chest, and his arm tightened around her protectively as they took off through the forest.

Into the horizon where their future awaited.

She savored the soft brush of Evren's thumb against her hand. She fought the sleep so desperately trying to take her for fear that when she drifted off, all she would see was the faces of the men she'd killed.

"I'm here Lu," Evren whispered against her ear. Her body relaxed the best it could.

"Evren," she whispered, her eyes drifting shut.

"Yes?"

"Are you taking me to Valebridge today?" She smiled at her poor joke, knowing his answer before he'd speak it.

Visions of ivy and hunters danced behind her eyelids. She was sore and tired, but being in his arms had already healed her.

He came for her. He saved her.

She saved herself.

Evren kissed her hair as their horse climbed a hill.

"No, Lu," he said. "Today I'll be taking you home."

EPILOGUE
FOUR YEARS LATER

"REALLY, LU? MORE IVY?" EVREN SHOOK HIS HEAD when he entered their shared room at the Jade Guild.

Tallulah laughed, her entire body shaking as she did. "I quite like it, don't you?"

She glanced around the room. The walls were now completely covered in the viny green foliage.

Evren joined her on the bed, shaking his head again.

"It's nostalgic." She winked.

"I like whatever you like." He kissed her quickly before pulling a book from the nightstand.

Tallulah smiled at him before returning her focus to the vines creeping over the ceiling.

She could hardly believe it'd been four years since they fled Davenport and showed up on Evren's uncle's doorstep. Four years since their life started at the Jade Guild. Four years since she took the lives of two men.

It hadn't been easy. In fact, much of it had been dreadful. His uncle wasn't happy to be harboring a fugitive of the kingdom. But as soon as he realized it meant Evren was home to stay, that Evren would take his place as Lord, his uncle's hate had lessened.

And over the years, slowly but surely, Tallulah and Thaddeus had formed a relationship of their own. Playing games of chess and giving Evren a hard time were just a few of the ways they enjoyed spending their evenings.

They were here, and they were safe.

Often, Tallulah ached for her greenhouse. For her magick she hadn't touched since the day she killed those men. But when she looked around at all the life she created with just her hands, she didn't feel as sad.

She shook off her thoughts and scooted toward Evren at the top of the bed. He bit his lip as he read his book, a habit he'd formed in the last few years. Smiling, she leaned in and kissed his neck. Then his ear. Then the freckles across his nose.

"Well, hello." He tossed the book to the side and pulled her onto his lap.

She laughed and wrapped her legs around him.

Sometimes she couldn't believe this was all real. That they were here, and he had chosen her. But when he looked at her with those eyes, with such passion, she couldn't imagine her life any other way. Guilt plagued her the first year they were here when Thaddeus locked up the Guild. But when she'd heard the other Guilds followed suit, locking their doors hoping to cut ties with King Roman, her guilt lessened. Now she was grateful for their refuge.

"Come here." Evren pulled her down into him.

Tallulah smiled just before his lips met hers. His tongue parted her lips, taking her for a deep kiss, and she moaned. Evren was a man of few words. But when he loved something, he *really* loved it.

And how lucky she felt to be the highest of his admirations.

Their kisses grew frenzied. Tallulah pulled for his shirt; all the while Evren clawed at her dress, pulling it over her head. He grabbed her breasts, his teeth grazing her neck.

She would never tire of this. Never tire of him and all the ways he made her feel whole.

And the best part, she would never have to.

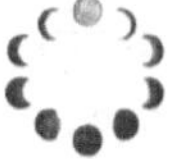

TALLULAH HAD DEVELOPED a bit of a snore since being here at the Jade Guild, but Evren chalked it up as her being comfortable for the first time in a long time.

He smiled at her sleeping and snoring as he bent down to search for his book. He found it buried under a pile of their discarded clothes. Hopping down, he slipped his breeches back on and grabbed his book before rejoining Lu on the bed to continue his reading.

He couldn't remember a time in his life he felt as good as this. As happy. Every day since they'd been here, fear was a constant companion. His mind often flashed to the day they'd fled. How broken she was. How close he was to losing her. The hurt in Markus' eyes when he realized his choice.

His eyes flicked to her again. She rolled away from him, letting out a sigh.

She was here. She was his.

He thought about Markus every day and even wrote him. But when he didn't get a response, he'd assumed Markus had left the country. Just as they'd always planned. It's a different kind of grief losing a friend. One that isn't as loud or spoken about, but Evren made his choice that day just as Markus had. And he'd do it again, because she was his world now.

Evren didn't intend to stay at the Jade Guild long. His plan was to heal Lu, keep quiet for a year or two, and then head for the docks once he could save up some coin. But something about being here lit Tallulah up. Her face beamed at all the glory of the forest and the flowers. Of the ivy that naturally grew here.

Many times, he thought about asking her to leave. To board a ship and start a new life. But every time he opened his mouth to suggest it, her blue eyes would catch his breath. And before he could speak, she would ramble on about a new species of flower she'd discovered growing in the Guild greenhouse.

He couldn't ask her to leave. Not when being here brought her so much joy. And since his uncle had turned around, Evren was no longer opposed to taking over duties as Lord when the time came.

Evren thumbed the pages of his book, glancing every few minutes to Tallulah. To make sure she was still here. Still safe.

He smiled again at his beautiful wife sleeping at his side. Her tan skin and strong jaw. Her soft lips and dark hair.

He tossed the book aside, abandoning his story to wrap his arms around her and join her in her slumber. He took a deep inhale of floral and vanilla as his body settled around hers.

A knock at the door drew his attention. Sighing, Evren leaned over to place a soft kiss on her temple so as not to wake her.

"I love you," he whispered. "More than all the stars."

He lazily pulled on his discarded shirt before opening the door.

"What is it?" he asked Henry, his mask still covering the lower part of his face.

"There's someone at the gate." Henry glanced past Evren for a moment to Tallulah. His dark eyes met Evren's again, his sandy hair spilling out from under his hood.

"You know what to do," Evren grumbled, ignoring the panic trickling into his bloodstream as it always did when someone showed up outside the Jade Guild walls.

It'd been years since the Jade Guild had locked up. No one came in, and only those on a supply run went out. Whenever an unwanted guest arrived, they did what they had to do. Evren turned, pulling the door shut behind him, but not before Henry's boot slipped out, stopping the door from closing.

"You're gonna want to talk to him," Henry said in a hushed tone.

Evren turned to face Henry again, his brows cinching together. "Why?"

He joined Henry in the hallway, closing the door to their bedroom behind him. It was unusual for the guards of the Jade Guild to approach Evren about an intruder. He'd trained them to handle such things. But Henry's insistence only made the panic clawing under Evren's skin more prominent.

"What business does he have?"

Henry took a steadying breath, his eyes shifting from Evren to the ground, then back to Evren. "Don't know, but he's claiming to be a Rudhek."

Evren's heart raced; the palms of his hands already slicked with sweat. "You're certain he said Rudhek?"

"Aye." Henry nodded, a grave expression passing over his face. "Says his name is Sorin."

Through a Somber Sky

Enchantress Awakens Book Two

See how it all ends, Fall 2024

Acknowledgments

Thank you so much for reading Tallulah and Evren's story! They hold such a special place in my heart. I can't wait for you to see what happens next. I owe quite a few people some thank yous, so bear with me here.

To my husband, for reminding me everyday that I can, in fact, do this.

To my editor, Brit, for challenging me. Pushing me. And most of all, *believing* in me. Without you, I'm certain these books wouldn't exist. I owe you so much.

To my family and friends, your support through this writing process has been unmatched.

To Katie, my ever faithful alpha reader. I'm not sure anyone loves Evren as much as you. (Maybe Tallulah. Maybe.)

To Lauren, for all your support through this entire process. I cherish your friendship so much.

To my beta team; Ash, Jenna, Krystal, and Sarah. Your help with this novella took it to the next level. Your words of encouragement and love for these characters gave me the motivation I needed to publish this story.

About Kristen

Kristen is a lifelong native to the Pacific Northwest, which is where most of her inspiration for writing comes from. She's been a lover of fantasy worlds for as long as she can remember. She and her husband live with their son and dog in Washington State. When she's not working, writing or chasing her toddler, you'll find her sipping coffee and exploring the woods or the nearby rivers. Through the Wicked Wood is her debut novel with many more to come.

More from Kristen

Enchantress Awakens

Through the Wicked Wood

As The Moon Falls

Through A Somber Sky (Fall 2024)

Seeds of Sorrow by Elle Beaumont & Christis Christie

Life for Eden is simple—until she's given to the nightmare king.

Wishing for more adventure in her life, and hoping to escape from under her overprotective mother's thumb even for just a night, Eden accepts an invitation to a ball in another king's court. Despite her mother's ire, it all seems worth it as their travels take Eden away from home for the first time and into the middle realm.

Draven, known as the king of nightmares and ruler of the dark realm, Andhera, desires only to remain in his kingdom and maintain control and order over the ravenous creatures that lurk in the shadows. However, he finds himself drawn away by the mysterious summons of his brother, who appears to need his aid desperately.

In one evening, thrust unwittingly together, Lady Eden and King Draven find themselves beguiled, betrayed, and betrothed. Neither is prepared for what it means for them, or for the immortal realms.

Available Now

*The Stars Would Curse Us by Stephanie Combs and Valerie
Rivers*

The Iris were sent to us from the stars, but their rule is controlling and oppressive. Every season, we send our brothers and sisters to the marriage drafts . . . but the selected never return.

Aella - My world falls apart when my best friend and I are drafted to compete for the hand of Esterra's most eligible bachelor, the devastatingly handsome Iris prince. As an elemental fae, it should be the greatest honor, but the competition is filled with violence. I question my true purpose as we fight to survive in games rigged against us.

Arianwen - Life should be simple—go on my rite and return to marry a man I've never met—but when a handsome stranger falls from the sky, everything is turned upside down. Secrets and lies unravel, leading me to question everything as I find myself pulled into a rebellion. My heart longs for a better world, but am I willing to forsake duty in pursuit of it?

We both face choices:

LOVE or DUTY

LOYALTY or ADVENTURE

FIGHT or SURRENDER

Is fate truly written in the stars, or have they abandoned us?

Available Now

The Songs That Beckon by M.A. Brown

Their grief binds them

The Song calls them

The Darkness wants to claim them

As winter wraps Areth in its frozen embrace, nightmarish beasts descend upon the Hastings household kidnapping Mr. and Mrs. Hastings and leaving behind their daughter, Bianca, as sole witness. In the wake of their abduction her quiet world is turned upside down and shaken revealing the secrets and lies her parents have buried.

As truths unravel it binds her to those who have similarly lost. Together they must wade through the thorny tangles of growing love and grief to find those that they hold dear before the looming threat of darkness is unleashed to destroy them all.

Travel worlds in this dark, dreamy and romantic debut filled with dusty books and pining looks.

Available Now